kids' guide
to the
internet

• Email the author
• Tell us your top ten sites
@ this book's very own website:
www.KidsInternet.dk.com

Dan Whitcombe

A Dorling Kindersley Book

Dorling Kindersley

LONDON, NEW YORK, SYDNEY, DELHI, PARIS
MUNICH, AND JOHANNESBURG

Project Editor Elinor Greenwood
Project Art Editors
Claire Penny, Jacqueline Gooden

Managing Editor Mary Ling
Managing Art Editor Rachael Foster
Production Kate Oliver
DTP Designer Almudena Díaz

First American Edition, 2000

00 01 02 03 04 05 10 9 8 7 6 5 4 3 2 1

Published in the United States by Dorling Kindersley Publishing, Inc.
95 Madison Avenue, New York, NY 10016

Copyright © 2000 Dorling Kindersley Limited

DK Publishing offers special discounts for bulk purchases for sales promotions or premiums.
Specific, large-quantity needs can be met with special editions, including personalized covers,
excerpts of existing guides, and corporate imprints. For more information, contact Special
Markets Department, DK Publishing, Inc., 95 Madison Avenue, New York, NY 10016.
Fax: (800) 600-9098.

ISBN 0-7894-7331-3

Color reproduction by Colourscan
Printed and bound by Graficas Estella, Spain.

Additional thanks to Susan Leonard and Samantha Gray for editorial assistance,
Marcus James for design assistance, and Chris Drew for jacket design.

See our complete
catalog at
www.dk.com

Tried and tested by Kids Domain

EVERY EFFORT HAS BEEN MADE TO ENSURE THAT THE INFORMATION
IN THIS BOOK IS AS UP-TO-DATE AS POSSIBLE AT THE TIME OF GOING
TO PRESS. THE INTERNET, BY ITS VERY NATURE, IS LIABLE TO CHANGE.
HOMEPAGE AND WEBSITE CONTENT IS CONSTANTLY BEING UPDATED,
AS WELL AS WEBSITE ADDRESSES. THE PUBLISHERS THEREFORE CANNOT
ACCEPT RESPONSIBILITY FOR ANY CONSEQUENCES ARISING FROM THE
USE OF THIS BOOK, OR GUARANTEE THAT THE WEBSITES AND URLS
WE FEATURE IN THIS BOOK WILL BE AS SHOWN.

CONTENTS

PARENTAL GUIDANCE   4-5
GOING PLACES   6-7

HOMEPAGES   8-9
SPEEDY BROWSING   10-11
SEARCH ENGINES   12-13

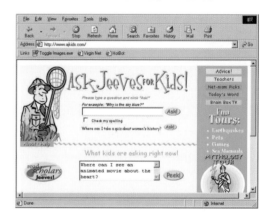

CREATING A WEBSITE   14-15
MAKING CONTACT   16-17

JUST FOR KIDS   18-19
GAME ON   20-23

SITES AND SOUNDS   24-27
SPORTING CHANCE   28-31

WORLD WATCH   48-51
SPACE   52-53

ANIMAL KINGDOM   32-35
WEB CRAWLERS   36-37

FUNNY OLD WORLD   54-55
HOMEWORK HELP   56-59

TIME TRAVEL   38-39
YOUR HISTORY   40-41

HOT SPOTS   60-61
NETSPEAK   62-63
THE FUTURE   64

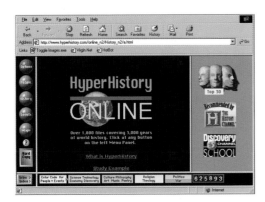

KEY

The symbols under each review in this book are ratings given to each website by the author. The more symbols, the better.

Spiders: a general review rating, ranging from 1-5

Lightning flashes: a rating for special effects, ranging from 1-5

Mortar boards: a rating for educational value, ranging from 1-3

PICTURE THIS   42-43
VIRTUAL GLOBETROTTER   44-47

PARENTAL GUIDANCE

If you've been around long enough to remember when mobile phones looked like doorstops, or your personal organizer was a battered book, then you'll know how quickly the cyberworld is developing. But if you don't know your psion from your i-book, or your email from your i-Mac, there's hope for you yet. Like every other technical advance, the internet might look complicated, but it's there to make your life easier.

http://microimg.com

HARD DRIVE SELL

In fact, one of the toughest parts of the whole process is buying the computer in the first place. Not only because the prices can be painful on the wallet, but also because there are so many to choose from. So, leaving the jargon-filled sales pitch aside, here are three pieces of advice to help you on your way to choosing the best computer for your money.

● Avoid frills. Concentrate on hard disk capacity, which should be at least 4 gigabytes (Gb), and short-term memory power (RAM) - 64 megabytes (Mb) should do the trick.

● For speedy surfing get a fast processor to optimize your modem connection. Like everything else in the cyberverse, things are getting faster all the time, and now there are lots of processors that offer over 600 Mhz of speed.

● It might sound like negative thinking, but find out how much it's going to cost to call the support hotline, and just what your warranty covers.

SIX STEPS TO CYBER HEAVEN

However good your choice, you still have to install the computer. You open the packaging to find: masses of anonymous boxes, an instruction manual comprising 15 languages with several different alphabet systems, and a labyrinth of technical jargon that would take a degree in information technology to decipher. You are probably familiar with the scenario. So, before you start to feel the whole thing's a big headache, here's a lightning guide to setup techniques.

● Clear a large work space near a multiplug socket.
● Put monitor (screen) on the desk and the central processing unit (CPU – the rectangular box!) under or next to it.
● Separate the cords that plug into the wall from the peripheral cables. The peripheral cables plug the printer, monitor, scanner, and so on, into the CPU; the wall sockets plug them into the wall.
● Insert "telephone" cable into the modem socket on the back of the CPU, and connect to your phone jack.
● TURN ON and insert the setup CD-rom.
● Follow user-friendly onscreen instructions.

Welcome to Larry's World

Get help online from Larry Magid.

www.larrysworld.com

SAFETY TIPS

Racism, violence, pornography, and even arms trading – no, the web is definitely not the safest of places. Part of the problem has been trying to censor material without coming across like Big Brother. Of course, talk of freedom of speech isn't much help if you're a worried parent just trying to ensure that your children don't inadvertently stumble on something unsuitable! But it isn't all bad news - you **can** make the internet safer.

DON'T PANIC!

For worried parents the key is to get involved in your kids' internet experience – explain the dangers and make sure they know not to give out personal details in chat rooms. Bookmark sites and search engines you approve of on your browser and, if you're still not satisfied, install a blocker or filter software (the free-to-download **We-Blocker** is a good place to start) which will cut out most of the web's more unsavory material.

Click on "How it works" for a full explanation of how to block websites with adult material.

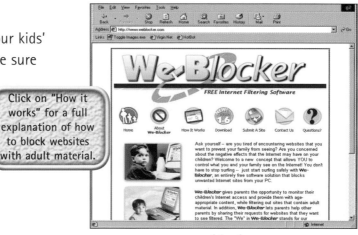

www.weblocker.com

SAFE AND FUN

But none of these systems are really foolproof. The fact is, parents can get left behind by their cyber-savvy youngsters. Stay a step ahead by visiting **Larry's World** (website address on opposite page). Larry gives tips on how to ensure safe surfing. He lists safe sites and search engines, and writes reviews on any new developments. He also includes links to sites with recommended software. **Kidsdomain** also gives a lot of good advice – as well as links to useful downloads like **Surfmonkey**.

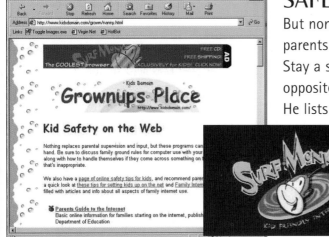

www.kidsdomain.com

www.surfmonkey.com

EAR TO THE GROUND

Parents can also try a cybersnooper – this is a version of the "History" tab built into modern browsers. **KidControl** (www.kidcontrol.com) takes regular snapshots of the pages your child is browsing, while **Cybersnoop 3.0** blocks and snoops email, chat, and newsgroups.

Click on "@ home" to view options.

www.pearlsw.com

HELP, NOT HINDRANCE

Kids aren't interested in most of the adult material online, because most of it either costs money or is about money, and stocks and pensions can be a definite turnoff. So in the long run this isn't really censorship, it's letting kids skip the junk and cut to the action.

GOING PLACES

Your computer has arrived, you've plugged it in, and you're ready to go. You've even got a strange device called a modem, and you're looking forward to your first time surfing the web. However, it doesn't seem to be as easy as you thought... how do you get to the internet? Why does nothing happen even though you're plugged into your phone connection? The internet can be a baffling place unless you know a few things before you get started. So before you throw down your mouse, follow our guide and your initiation to surfing the web will be a happy and hazard-free experience.

AT YOUR SERVICE

Although the web is often compared to a library with millions of pages of information, the whole internet works a little like a telephone network. To get online your computer needs to tap into the network by dialing a number on its modem. To do this you need an **Internet Service Provider (ISP)** or Online Service, whose job is something like that of a telephone company. They are the first stage in the journey onto the web, telling your computer what number it needs to dial every time you want to send an email or surf the internet.

THE RIGHT ISP

There are a lot of ISPs, and choosing the right one is very important. They are your main link to the internet, and provide you with the passwords you need to log on. The biggest companies in the US are AOL, WorldCom, MSN, EarthLink, and RCN.

JUST BROWSING

Once the ISP has given you a password to cyberspace, what you need is a tour guide to show you around. With millions of new sites appearing all the time, the web is not somewhere you want to get lost! That's where browsers come in handy. Browsers are computer packages or programs you install which help the computer to work effectively. Browsers speak the same language, or "protocol," as the web. The internet uses a language that is made up of a series of signs and arrows, and the browser acts as a speedy interpreter so you can read the webpages.

MAJOR PLAYERS

Two internet giants, Netscape and Microsoft, have cornered the browser market; and, as their programs are constantly being improved, the latest Netscape Navigator or Internet Explorer packages are probably the best.

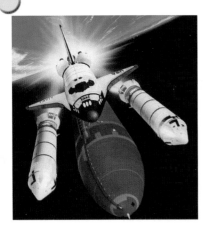

SEARCH ME!

Now you've got your connection to the web and a tour guide to help you get around, what you really need is some form of transportation. This is where search engines come in. There are hundreds to choose from and they all seem similar, but choosing a search engine is like catching a taxi – they all look the same, but some drivers are much better than others. What you need is one that knows all the shortcuts and isn't afraid to step on the gas! See pages 12-13 for a definitive list of the very best search engines.

HOMEPAGE BOUND

If you're using the right search engine, you should soon arrive at your destination – the website itself. A website is a little like a house – it has its own address, or URL, which is what you give your taxi driver, and a homepage that is the front door to the site, welcoming you in and telling you what to expect inside. Of course, once you're there, there are lots of rooms, or webpages, behind the homepage that contain different features. However, even though the search engine can get you there, you need help to move from room to room...

HYPERLINKS

Now you need the final tool in your web traveling kit – the hyperlink. This is much simpler than it sounds. When you are on the web you will notice all kinds of buttons and highlighted words. If you pass your cursor over one of these and it turns into a hand, then it's a hyperlink.

Click on any of the tabs at the side of the page and take a shortcut to the site's highlights.

http://disney.co.uk/disneyonline/safesurfing/index.html

SAFE SURFING

Even when you're a whiz at finding your way around the web, there are still lots of tips you need to pick up to make your surfing safer. For a fun guide to supersurfing, take a look at the **Disney Online** "Doug's safe surfing tips" (shown above). He's got lots of helpful hints and some great hyperlinks to games – also check out the "CyberNetiquette Comix."

HOMEPAGES

Every website has a homepage. It is like the contents page of a book, telling you what you can find on the website. There are two types of websites: "portals," which are websites with links to other sites (search engines come under this category), and websites that do not have links to other sites, such as the DK site. The DK homepage acts as a gateway to the contents of the site, while a search engine homepage acts as a gateway out into the whole of cyberspace.

▶ HOMING IN

Take a look at the **Yahooligans!** homepage (this is a very useful search engine – see pages 11-12). To get to it, you type the website address in the space below the toolbar and hit "Return." Then follow the tips in the buttons to move around.

The toolbar lets you go forward and back, saves your favorite sites, and remembers where you've been (see page 10 for more info).

These tabs are links to all the site's special features.

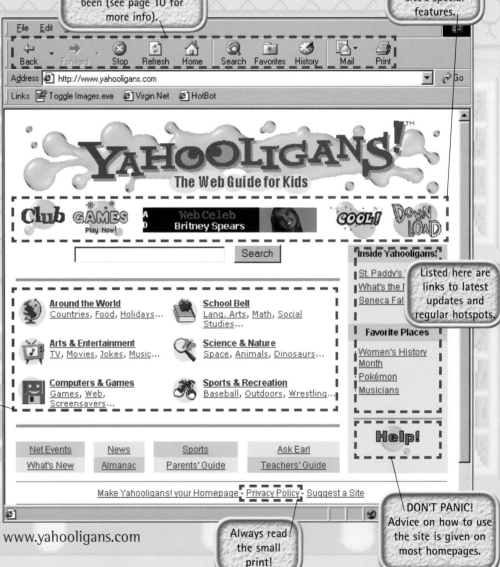

www.yahooligans.com

This is a search engine, so it has a directory of the entire web. On other homepages, the directory of the site is here.

Listed here are links to latest updates and regular hotspots.

DON'T PANIC! Advice on how to use the site is given on most homepages.

Always read the small print!

TOP TIP
To make your favorite site the first homepage you see each time you access the internet, click on "Preferences," then "Home," and enter the address of the page you want.

DK.COM

Not all homepages look the same. Yahooligans! is a search engine so it takes you to lots of other sites. Most homepages are not so ambitious. They merely tell you what's in the website. Take the **DK.com** site, for example. Its homepage tells you where to find out about all its new books and multimedia products. You can click on tabs or key words under the particular headings that interest you. For example, you'll find "Build your own website!" under "DK for kids."

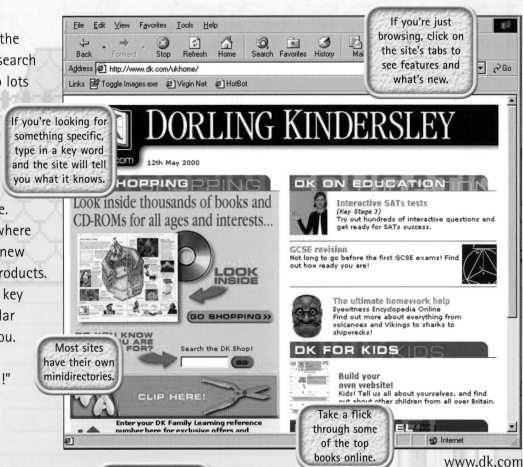

If you're looking for something specific, type in a key word and the site will tell you what it knows.

If you're just browsing, click on the site's tabs to see features and what's new.

Most sites have their own minidirectories.

Take a flick through some of the top books online.

www.dk.com

This homepage has some neat gimmicks. Run your cursor across the Japanese writing for an instant translation.

This homepage has lots of links to games, as well as fun paper-folding activities.

Why not enter the ThinkQuest contest next year? Start with our tips for making your own website on pages 14-15.

http://tqjunior.thinkquest.org/5402

HOMEMADE

But if it's fun surfing you're after, then maybe directory portals and commercial homepages are not what you want. Not all websites are created by big organizations – anyone can do it with a little know-how. Here is the homepage of a website that won an annual competition run by **ThinkQuest Junior** last year. The kids that made this have proved that there is more to Origami than making paper airplanes.

SPEEDY BROWSING

Have you ever wondered how many sites there are on the web? No one knows for sure, although it is certain that there are tens, if not hundreds, of millions, with new sites being added all the time. That's what makes it such an exciting place. However, it also means that for every site worth its weight in cyber gold, there are many that don't make the grade. Time spent online costs money and, with a wealth of websites to choose from, it's worth noting some practical hints to speed up your browsing.

► USING BROWSER TOOLS

If you use your browser effectively, it can speed up your searches drastically. Remember the hints given here, and after a little practice you will soon be whizzing around the web like an expert.

If a page is very slow to load, it's often best to try another option. Don't spend hours waiting – just hit the "Stop" button and then click on "Back."

Click on the "Favorites" or "Bookmark" icon on your browser and then "Add" to store the addresses of your favorite sites. This allows you to find them quickly.

You can find your favorites even more quickly if you "Organize" them into folders.

Click on "History" in the toolbar to remember all the websites you have looked up in the past few weeks.

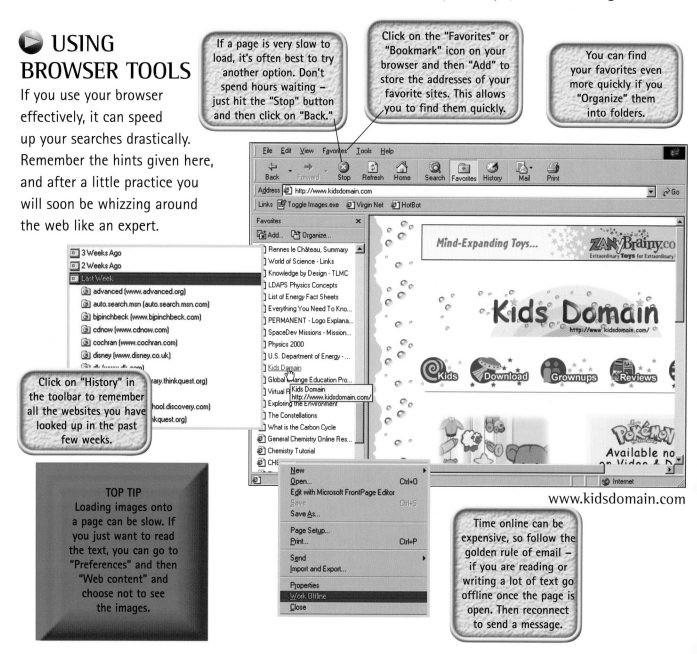

www.kidsdomain.com

TOP TIP
Loading images onto a page can be slow. If you just want to read the text, you can go to "Preferences" and then "Web content" and choose not to see the images.

Time online can be expensive, so follow the golden rule of email – if you are reading or writing a lot of text go offline once the page is open. Then reconnect to send a message.

SURF WIZARDS

There are millions of sites and hundreds of thousands of cyber dead ends, so finding your way around quickly is going to take a little more than just knowing a few crafty shortcuts. What you need is a good driver that knows the way around and can save you from taking any time-wasting wrong turns. This is where search engines can take you supersonic!

▶ THE RIGHT QUESTION

Search engines help to find things when you don't know a specific address. You can find a guide to the best engines on the next page; but, before you dive straight in, you need to know a little about how they work. You might remember that search engines are like taxis – some are faster than others, but even with the best taxi driver, it's helpful to give detailed instructions about where you want to go. So when you're typing in what you're looking for, be as clear as possible to give the search engine a really good chance of finding it.

www.google.com

Fans of the Spice Girls should remember not to type in just "spice" if they don't want pages of curry recipes!

ADVANCE TO GO

True search maestros can graduate to an advanced search. Lots of the best engines let you speed up your search by only displaying sites from a certain date, or with specific types of pictures or animation, or for users of a particular age. This could save you hours of wading through stuff you don't need later on.

◀ HOW CAN I HELP YOU?

If you don't have a specific destination in mind, then things can be even harder. That's why lots of search engines give you guidance in case you can't think of a key word to type in. Some of the biggest engines, like Yahoo!, Altavista, and Lycos have really good category searches that let you narrow down your search to the right kind of website – science, education, sports, entertainment, and so on. Using these categories can help to speed up your searches.

www.yahoo.com

SEARCH ENGINES

If you've tried all the tips and asked all the right questions and you still can't find what you're looking for, then perhaps you're using the wrong search engine. If knowing how to phrase your question can speed up your search, then knowing your top 10 search engines, and what their strengths and weaknesses are, can take you into turbodrive. Read on to find out more about the best search engines on the web.

▶ GO FOR IT

The **goto.com** homepage is a beautifully simple word search engine. It will trawl the internet and come up with some great sites. All you have to do is type in your key words, and sit back while it goes to work.

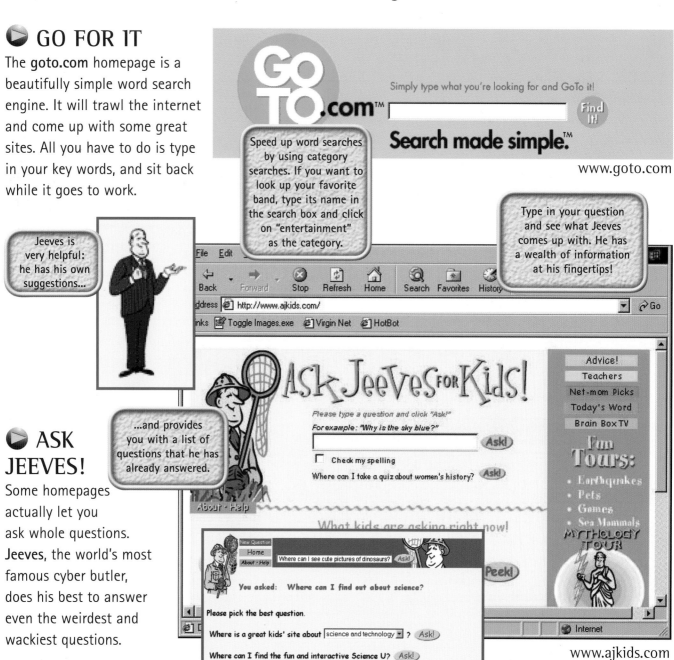

Speed up word searches by using category searches. If you want to look up your favorite band, type its name in the search box and click on "entertainment" as the category.

Simply type what you're looking for and GoTo it!

Search made simple.™

www.goto.com

Type in your question and see what Jeeves comes up with. He has a wealth of information at his fingertips!

Jeeves is very helpful: he has his own suggestions...

...and provides you with a list of questions that he has already answered.

▶ ASK JEEVES!

Some homepages actually let you ask whole questions. **Jeeves**, the world's most famous cyber butler, does his best to answer even the weirdest and wackiest questions.

Ask Jeeves for Kids!

Please type a question and click "Ask!"
For example: "Why is the sky blue?"

☐ Check my spelling

Where can I take a quiz about women's history? Ask!

About · Help

What kids are asking right now!

Advice!
Teachers
Net-mom Picks
Today's Word
Brain Box TV

Fun Tours:
• Earthquakes
• Pets
• Games
• Sea Mammals
MYTHOLOGY TOUR

New Question
Home
About · Help

Where can I see cute pictures of dinosaurs? Ask!

You asked: Where can I find out about science?

Please pick the best question.

Where is a great kids' site about science and technology ? Ask!

Where can I find the fun and interactive Science U? Ask!

www.ajkids.com

WEB WATCH

Other good search engines:

www.beritsbest.com

www.KidsClick.com

www.yahooligans.com

www.about.com

www.altavista.com

www.google.com

www.infoseek.com

www.excite.com

Huge databases:

www.encyberpedia.com

www.britannica.com

⏵ QUESTION TIME

Other cyber gurus think about your question and then email you the answer, or post it up on the site's bulletin board. One of the best is **Dr. Universe**; but don't expect him to get back to you immediately – he is under a lot of pressure!

See how the website works by clicking on "How can I submit my question."

www.wsu.edu/DrUniverse

The best thing about some of the kids' searchers is that they also give the sites a fun and educational rating.

⏵ COOL FOR KIDS

There are also some specialized kid engines – so you don't have to worry about pages and pages of advanced astrophysics. Two of the best are **Yahooligans!** and **Lycos Zone**; but if you're new to the web, try **Berit's Best Sites for Kids** or **KidsClick** (see above box for URLs), and you'll soon get the picture.

www.lycoszone.com

www.dogpile.com

Metasearch engines might not be quick, but if the answer is out there, they'll find it in the end.

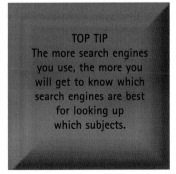

TOP TIP
The more search engines you use, the more you will get to know which search engines are best for looking up which subjects.

⏶ WEB JUNGLE KINGS

If all else fails you can fall back on one of the mighty metasearchers - the web surveillance engines that know what other searchers have on their files. Some of them use hundreds of other search engines. Try **Dogpile.com**, which has a great directory of subjects, and is particularly speedy.

CREATING A WEBSITE

One of the most exciting aspects of the internet is that it is great for communicating with other people from all over the world. A good way of making contact is to set up your own website and let other internet users come to you. It's surprisingly simple to do, and once you know how, you can tell the world all about your favorite films, games, and hobbies – as well as your pet peeves.

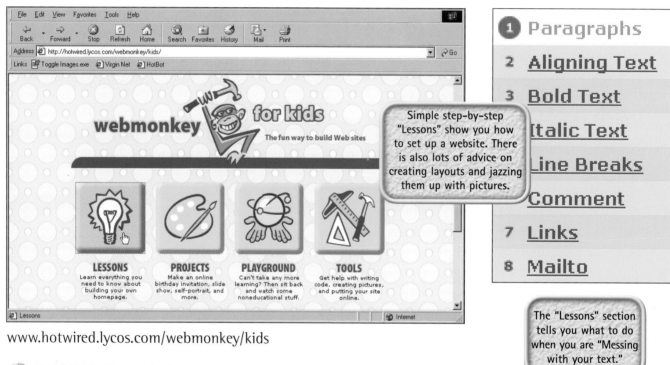

www.hotwired.lycos.com/webmonkey/kids

Simple step-by-step "Lessons" show you how to set up a website. There is also lots of advice on creating layouts and jazzing them up with pictures.

The "Lessons" section tells you what to do when you are "Messing with your text."

MONKEY BUSINESS

Creating your own website is easier than you might think. There are fantastic websites dedicated to showing you how, and an especially good one is **Webmonkey for kids**. Start by clicking on "Lessons," and once you've mastered the basics, move on to "Projects" for tips on what you can use a website for. To see some wonderful web ideas, click on "Playground." "Tools" will give you links to other useful websites.

JARGON-BUSTING

A lot of the jargon used in setting up websites can make the process look more complicated than it really is. Here are a couple of common abbreviations: HTML (HyperText Markup Language) is information written in code that you give to the computer so that it knows what it's supposed to do. FTP (File Transfer Protocol) is the way the computer sends files over the internet. It is the particular mail service the browser uses to put your page online (or "upload").

TOP TIP
To see what the HTML code looks like on the page you're on, click on "View" then "Source" (or "Page source") on your browser toolbar.

HOW COOL IS YOUR SCHOOL?

Why not put your school on the internet? Team up with some classmates and set up a school website. Top-of-the-class websites have interesting text, great pictures, quick links, and excellent icons. Your school site could feature pictures of the school, your teachers, and classmates. Let the world know what's special about your school!

At this school site you can listen to ex-pupils performing their own song.

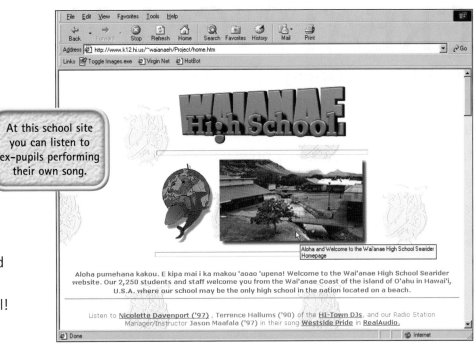

www.k12.hi.us/~waianaeh/Project/home.htm

www.websitegarage.com

TUNE IN, TUNE UP

Once your website is up and running, the job's still not over. A website is like a machine, and it needs to be kept in good working condition. At the **Website Garage**, you can submit your site for a free "tune up," find out how to maximize the number of visitors to your site, and speed up image download.

Click on "Hitometer" to learn how to keep track of your website traffic.

CYBERBEE

Join the **CyberBee**'s "Guide for making a school homepage" and he'll show you around some of the best homepages. The CyberBee also gives useful advice on putting a site together, such as keeping your message clear and remembering who your target audience is.

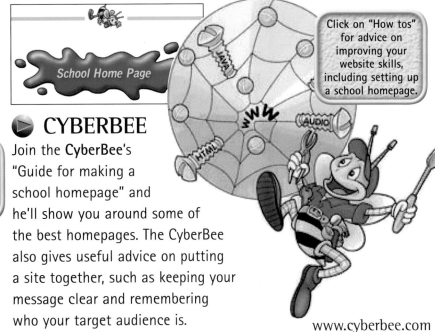

Click on "How tos" for advice on improving your website skills, including setting up a school homepage.

www.cyberbee.com

WHERE'S HOME?

Once you have set up your website, you will need a place to keep it on the internet. To find out about the many options available, visit **Free Web Space (www.freewebspace.net)**. Alternatively, you can start with either **www.tripod.com** or **www.geocities.com**

MAKING CONTACT

Email allows you to communicate with people across the world instantly through the internet. Sending a message is as easy as mailing a letter – only much faster! Email lets you send letters and documents, and you can even access your mail from other computers. To make sure that only you can open your mail, you need a password. This should have a limited number of characters, and be a word you can remember!

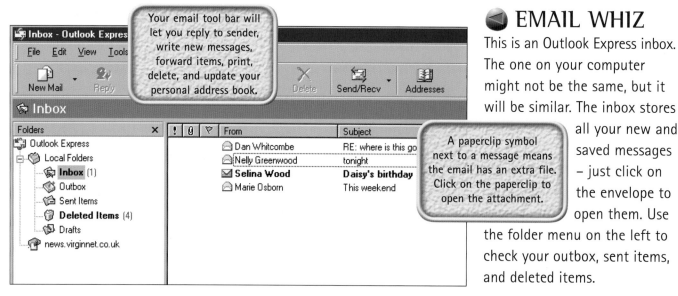

Your email tool bar will let you reply to sender, write new messages, forward items, print, delete, and update your personal address book.

A paperclip symbol next to a message means the email has an extra file. Click on the paperclip to open the attachment.

EMAIL WHIZ

This is an Outlook Express inbox. The one on your computer might not be the same, but it will be similar. The inbox stores all your new and saved messages – just click on the envelope to open them. Use the folder menu on the left to check your outbox, sent items, and deleted items.

ADDRESS BOOKS

The address book stores the email addresses of the people you contact most often. You simply click on the name in your address book, rather than typing in the address every time. The easiest way to add new addresses to the folder is by importing them from sent messages. The process for doing this varies, but can be as simple as double clicking on the sender's name.

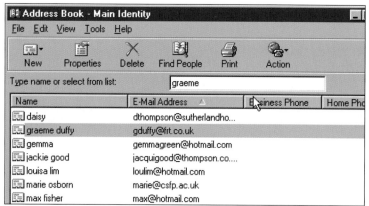

THE WEBMAIL OPTION

Fed up with hiding your emails from snooping brothers and sisters? You can bypass the ISP (Internet Service Provider) or browser mail software by setting up a free webmail account. It is usually slower to get your mail this way because you have to go through the web. On the positive side, you can access your mail from any computer with an internet connection. Go to the Hotmail (**www.hotmail.com**) or Rocket Mail (**www.rocketmail.com**) sites to find out more.

MAIL ORDER

Although an email software program often comes with an ISP or online service, your browser might have its own mail package. Recent versions of Netscape mostly have the **Messenger** mail program or, in the case of Microsoft, a version of **Outlook Express**. To open your account you may need to go through a process called "configuration." This is much simpler than it sounds! The webpage wizard provides a simple, online template where you enter your personal details and chosen password, and the program itself takes you step by step through all the stages of setting up the account.

NETIQUETTE

For emails, chat forums, and newsgroups, there is a language system called "netiquette." This uses abbreviations, such as "KISS" (keep it short and simple), as well as a variety of fun symbols to help you get your message across. Here are a few of the most popular ones to start with:

:-) just kidding!

:-o you can't be serious!

\o/ hip hip hurray!

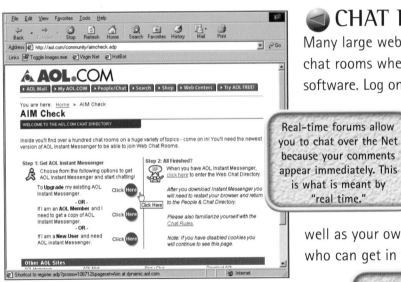

http://aol.com

Real-time forums allow you to chat over the Net because your comments appear immediately. This is what is meant by "real time."

CHAT ROOMS

Many large websites and online services have their own chat rooms where you will find easy-to-download chat software. Log on to the homepage of AOL, for example, and click on to the chat icon. There is a download wizard that provides you with **AOL Instant Messenger** for free. This is one of the best ways of experiencing chat online. AOL gives you access to real-time forums as well as your own set of options, so you can decide who can get in touch with you and when.

TALKING PAGES

Most kids' chat sites work in much the same way. To begin, you have to register as a member, with a nickname, or "handle," and a password. Many sites also ask for your parents' email address so that they can check that you have permission to use the site. Once you have registered, you are set to log on and find a good chat room.

Follow KidsCom's advice – "Play smart, stay safe, have fun."

www.kidscom.com

Click on the "Graffiti wall" at Kidscom and chat with kids from all over the world.

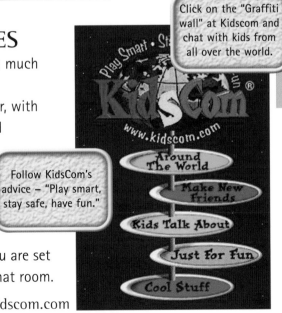

Send C-cards

Graffiti Wall Chat

TOP TIP
Some chat services still ask you to install a plug-in, but many will now work without one as long as you are using a browser that can handle Java.

JUST FOR KIDS

There are so many good websites for that dull afternoon that it's difficult to know where to begin. However, a visit to FreeZone for Kids will provide a great chat and games experience, and Headbone Zone is pretty amazing too. In fact, if you visit the sites featured on these pages, you're guaranteed to have so much fun that you'll lose all track of time. So check them out and say goodbye to boredom forever!

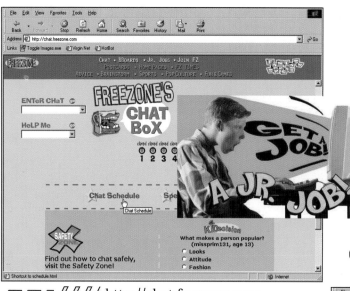

 http://chat.freezone.com

▶ HEAD TO HEAD

If you liked FreeZone, then you'll love **Headbone Zone**. There's more than enough to keep anyone busy on a dull day. Apart from loads of chat rooms, there are also 24-hour game rooms, where you can pit your skills against other players in real-time competition. You can also get advice on all areas of your life from Velma in the "What's up?" section.

www.headbone.com/splash.html

◀ FUN ZONE

There's lots to do on **FreeZone for Kids** – a fully-monitored chat zone with only quality material. Check out "Brain storm" for some homework help, or look for a job with "Jr. Jobs." For any budding reporters and writers, subscribe to the "FZ Times" where you can send in your own stories. But if it's games you're after, then "Create-a-creature," "Whack-an-elf," or feed the "Gag-o-matic" your favorite one-liners.

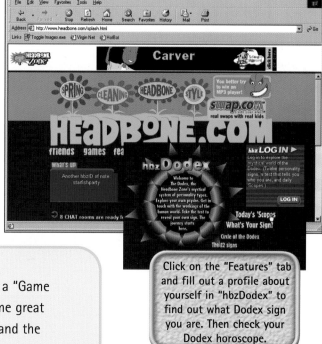

WEB WATCH
KidsCom is a great site with lots of games and a "Game pad" bulletin board where you can pick up some great cheats. It's also the home of "Find a key pal" and the "Graffiti wall chat." **www.KidsCom.com**

Click on the "Features" tab and fill out a profile about yourself in "hbzDodex" to find out what Dodex sign you are. Then check your Dodex horoscope.

☎ ⚡⚡⚡⚡ www.mamamedia.com/home.html

MAMMA MIA!

MaMaMedia is an excellent site that will defy you to get bored. It is packed with dozens of games, activities, and puzzles. Enter by clicking on "Play" and then take potluck at "Surprise" or design your own "Presto" town that will go online for other surfers to inspect. You can also animate some wacky characters in "Frame that toon," then do some crazy painting at "Kids web paint."

🕷 🕷 🕷 🕷

Visit "Zap" on the homepage and design your own MaMaMedia screen.

WEB WATCH

You'll be dumbfounded at **Stupid.com**. Subscribe to the "Stupid newsletter," or have a go at "Stinko-pachinko." There's a "Random stupid joke" server, and a game where you use your cursor to try and squish bugs that move around the screen.

www.stupid.com

☎ ☎ ☎ ⚡⚡⚡⚡ www.yucky.com

GROSS ENCOUNTERS

If you like worms, then **Yucky.com** is the place for you! "Yucky fun and games" has regularly updated activities you can try out. You can knock up some "Revolting recipes," or "Icky experiments" featuring Vampire Soap and Mighty Morphin' Milk. 🕷 🕷 🕷 🕷

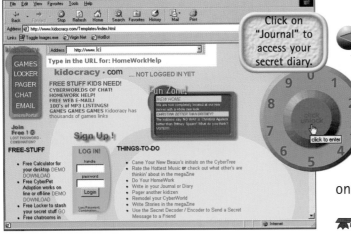

Click on "Journal" to access your secret diary.

KIDS RULE!

This isn't a democracy, it's a kidocracy! So join your fellow kidizens at **Kidocracy.com**, where you can chat in your own cyberworlds, and make up your own rules. Once you've logged on, there are loads of chats, votes, polls, and a good webzine. You also get your own secret locker that only you have the combination to. 🕷 🕷 🕷 🕷

☎ ☎ ⚡⚡⚡ www.kidocracy.com

GAME ON

Think of a game – any game – and you'll find it online. Take your pick from thousands of downloadable demos of the latest video, interactive, and real-time multiplayer games. You can also test your brain, nerve, and quick reactions against the computer in some of the fastest online mind games. And don't forget to visit the sites that tell you what's new, so you stay ahead of the crowd.

If you have any trouble playing the games, just click on "Help." Easy-to-follow instructions help you to figure out problems – and to get on with having fun.

www.javagameplay.com

ACTION-PACKED

For great, all-action games that don't need plug-ins or downloads and are totally free of charge (except the telephone charges, of course!), visit **Javagameplay.com**. These games can be played as long as your web browser supports Java. Test your skill with games such as "Alien invasion" and "Orbital defense." With one million visitors to this site in six months, it must be worth a look!

BONUS GAME

If you're new to online games, **Bonus.com** is a great place to start. This site is an excellent introduction to the world of game playing, with levels for all ages and skills. Choose from aliens, mazes, monsters, sports, and multiplayer games, to name a few. You'll find that they're all quick to load. The site also has regular competitions with prizes for the winners.

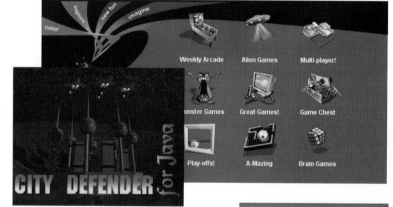

www.bonus.com

WEB WATCH

Even if you have favorite console gizmos (the computer accessories for games), it's worth checking out the **Nintendo** or **Playstation** websites (see this page's border for URLs). They give useful information, budget tips, and special offers on gizmos.

TOP TIP
Take a sneaky peek at CheatElite and get ahead of yourself!
www.cheatelite.com

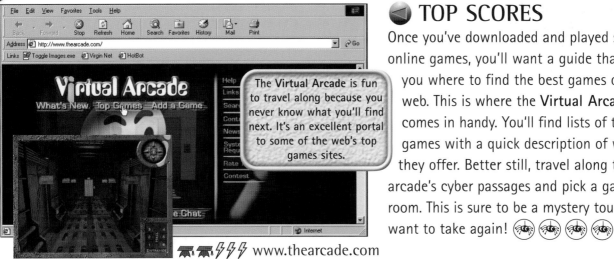

> The **Virtual Arcade** is fun to travel along because you never know what you'll find next. It's an excellent portal to some of the web's top games sites.

TOP SCORES

Once you've downloaded and played some online games, you'll want a guide that shows you where to find the best games on the web. This is where the **Virtual Arcade** comes in handy. You'll find lists of the top games with a quick description of what they offer. Better still, travel along the arcade's cyber passages and pick a games room. This is sure to be a mystery tour you'll want to take again!

www.thearcade.com

GAME PLAN

If you are searching for the ultimate online gaming experience, log on at **Zeeks.com**. They've got dozens of arcade, board, and educational games as well as a gang of friendly cyber gamesters that are on call to make your time online more fun. Click onto "Matt's" link for loads of gaming tips, or chill out at "Nikki's place." Once you've mastered all the games at Zeeks, visit the "Surfshack" for links to other top games sites.

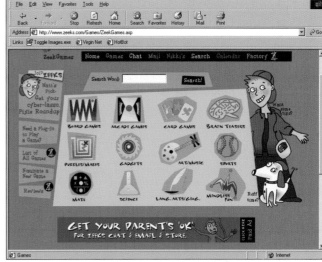

www.zeeks.com/Games

> Before you start playing, choose a name that suits your gaming style from the list. Then play the games in character.

BRAIN TEASERS

To get your brain cells working, visit the **Yahoo!** and **Yahooligans!** game zones, where you'll find some great brain teasers such as checkers, chess, and word searches, as well as tricky mazes and puzzles.

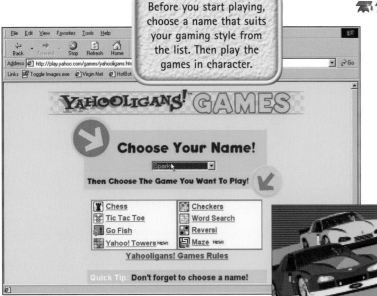

http://games.yahoo.com/games/yahooligans.html

WEB WATCH

Yahoo!'s games are all free and you don't need to spend time downloading plug-ins. You just need to make sure your browser handles Java.

http://games.yahoo.com

BRAIN GAMES

Playing online doesn't have to mean the latest in video game technology. There are great sites to test your mind and reflexes at **Bonnie's Games.** Most require either Java or Shockwave, but they're all handpicked and you can choose games to match your level of skill. Try saving the world from low-quality pizza at **Tony's pizza game**, or test your brain power at the **Web puzzler.**

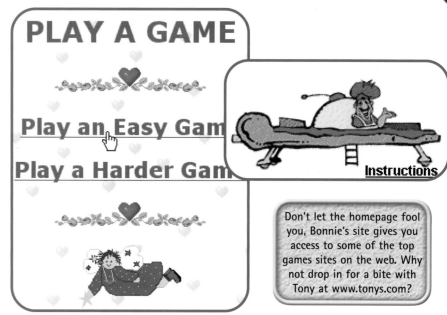

PLAY A GAME

Play an Easy Game

Play a Harder Game

Instructions

Don't let the homepage fool you, Bonnie's site gives you access to some of the top games sites on the web. Why not drop in for a bite with Tony at www.tonys.com?

www2.arkansas.net/~mom/game.html

Forensic Files - Case 001!

ON THE CASE

If you prefer testing your mental agility to action and adventure games, visit the "Forensic files" at **Discover learning.** Budding detectives can try out their powers of deduction by teaming up with Newton Beagle, the canine supersleuth, to travel the world and solve mysteries. Newton will give you clues to follow up, and you decide whether to interrogate witnesses and suspects along the way.

www.discoverlearning.com/forensic/docs

CAT IN THE HAT

Join the "Cat in the Hat," and a cast of other characters, in **Seussville**. Click on "Shockwave games" to test your wits in the "Cat's concentration game," play the "Sneetch belly game" with Sylvester McBean, or help the teachers find their classrooms in "Hooray for Diffendoofer Day."

WEB WATCH

Young entrepreneurs can try out their business skills at the **Lemonade Stand**. Maybe you can make a cool, refreshing million?

www.littlejason.com/lemonade/

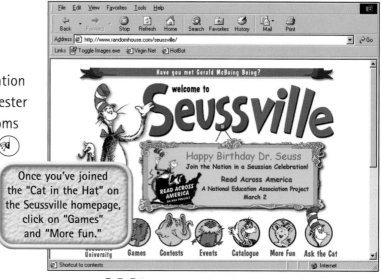

Once you've joined the "Cat in the Hat" on the Seussville homepage, click on "Games" and "More fun."

www.randomhouse.com/seussville

ANIMATED ACTION

For fantastic animation, visit **Disney**'s games site and click on the type of game you want to play. You may have to download a plug-in, but it's worth the wait. Disney updates its games to include cartoon heroes from its recent movie releases, so check out the "What's new" section and try "Tigger bounce" and "Cruella drive" for some up-to-date cartoon mayhem.

Try the "Football competition" – and help Mickey Mouse score as many goals as possible in 90 seconds.

http://disney.co.uk/DisneyOnline/Games

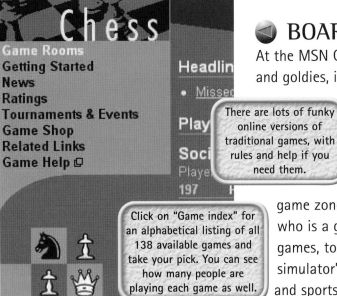

Click on "Game index" for an alphabetical listing of all 138 available games and take your pick. You can see how many people are playing each game as well.

There are lots of funky online versions of traditional games, with rules and help if you need them.

www.zone.com

BOARD OF PLAYING?

At the MSN Gaming Zone, you'll find a great selection of oldies and goldies, including backgammon, blackjack, card games, checkers, and chess, as well as Battleship, Monopoly, and Pictionary. With these board games, you don't have to worry about putting all the pieces back in the box afterward, or finding someone to play with! The different multiplayer game zones mean you can choose your room and play someone who is a good match for you. There are lots of single-player games, too. Try the great simulation games, such as "Flight simulator" and "Top gun," and move on to the fantastic action and sports games for even more excitement.

WORD PERFECT!

If you're a top-class wordsmith, test your skills at **Scrabble.com**. Click on "For kids eyes only" to play the "Scrabble snake" game, "Scrabble hangman," or test your speed on the spelling draw with "Scrabble invaders." You can also click on "Tips" to improve your word skills.

www.scrabble.com

TOP TIP
If you're an avid Monopoly player, visit Monopoly.com for some tournament news and fun facts. Check out the "Strategy wizard" for tips on how to make the best deals and own all that hot property!
www.monopoly.com

SITES AND SOUNDS

Sometimes it's hard to keep up with the stars – one day the newspapers say that your favorite movie star is getting married, the next getting divorced! But it is possible to keep your finger on the pulse of the film and music world's top celebs without joining the paparazzi. These websites ensure that you'll be well-informed about all the gossip.

HOLLYWOOD THRILLS

There are lots of sites that let you into the lives of the rich and famous, with all the news and gossip. There are even celebrity chat forums where you can chat with stars online. Up there with the best is the **Teenhollywood** website where you'll find contests, quizzes, and features from top cyber reporters. All the latest films are reviewed and the stars interviewed, and there's gossip about pop stars too. So if you want to know when your favorite pop group is releasing a new album, or who is up for an Oscar, this is the place to find out.

> All the latest news and gossip, plus the week's top celebs. "Pick a celebrity" and link up with up-and-coming teenage stars.

www.teenhollywood.com

> Click on "Features" and read the movie previews and Mr. Showbiz interviews with celebrities. Look at the photo gallery and see the stars all decked out for the Oscars.

STAR GAZERS!

If Teenhollywood is the place to go to get all the latest news and gossip, you can't beat **Mr. Showbiz** for star ratings. He's the media detective who's got celeb files on anyone you could want to check up on. And not just the latest stuff either – you can open a file on a star, current or past, and find a whole archive of photos, interviews, and interesting facts.

www.mrshowbiz.com

> If you want to step up the pace, then click on the "Music" tab and check out the "Wall of sound," Mr. Showbiz's music chart listings, with RealPlayer videos of all the latest hits.

NICK'S PICK

If gossip leaves you reaching for your mouse, then head straight for the on-screen action itself. And what better place than the **Nickelodeon** homepage. This site has great links to all their programs, so you can meet up with Ren and Stimpy or Tommy Pickles and the rest of the Rugrats. Pick up your backstage pass for the latest gossip and "Nicksclusives," or relax in the game zone with SpongeBob.

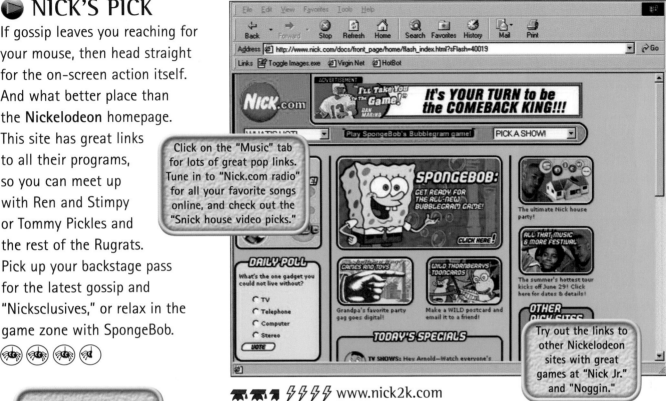

Click on the "Music" tab for lots of great pop links. Tune in to "Nick.com radio" for all your favorite songs online, and check out the "Snick house video picks."

Try out the links to other Nickelodeon sites with great games at "Nick Jr." and "Noggin."

www.nick2k.com

For more fun and games, click on the "Web premiere toons" link for some great interactive movies and original clips.

http://cartoonnetwork.com/doc/texavery/index.html

ANIMATED ACTION

Don't get lost trying to find a site where you can hang out with all your screen heroes, especially if they're of the superhero cartoon variety. Get animated down at the **Cartoon Network Dept. of Cartoons** site to view some great video clips from the golden age of animation. Brush up on cartoon history, and find out just how the artists work to put together your favorite wacky toon adventures at "Background" and "Viewing cards."

WEB WATCH

For more comic fun that you can really get involved in, visit the **Cartoon Corner**, and pick up all the tricks of the trade.

www.cartooncorner.com

▶ DISNEY WORLD

You've already seen it on the Cartoon Network, and there's more proof of it at **Disney.com** – you don't need to be real to be a superstar! So if you're fed up with real-life celebrities and spoiled prima donnas, join the cartoon folk and your favorite Disney characters for bundles of freewheeling fun, activities, games, comics, and cool graphics at "Club Blast."

Tune in to the "Disney Channel" for lots of interactive activities – enter the "Sound booth," play the "Shrinking game," or join Mickey for a Paris adventure.

Click on "Films" for info on all Disney's new releases.

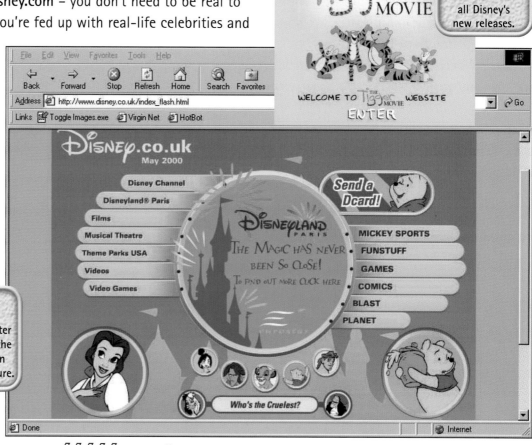

www.disney.com

▶ IT'S BEHIND YOU!

With the amazing special effects on offer at **Imax**, scary monsters could be lurking behind you, as well as above, below, in front, and to the side of you! Imax has put together a site that shows you the technological stunts they can pull off. Go backstage and learn about what goes into making an Imax 3-D movie. If normal film effects make you jump, you'd better be careful!

Click on "Innovations" for different types of Imax films.

Get all the latest information about Imax films now showing, and the ones coming soon.

www.imax.com

WEB WATCH

For more animation mayhem, check out the **Cartoon Network**'s games, where you can play games with toon stars such as Scooby Doo, Bugs Bunny, and Fred Flintstone.

http://cartoonnetwork.com/games/index.html

MUSICAL INTERLUDE

If flashing lights and special effects have left your head spinning, then maybe what you need is a little light music to get your feet tapping. Make your way down to the orchestra pit at **Play Music**, and find out all about how each of the musical instruments makes the sounds you hear – and just how they work together to create a full orchestra effect. When you've got the hang of that, you can go backstage and take up the challenge of a musical play-off against Molly, where you get a chance to perform yourself.

> In level three, click on a record of your choice (so it's on top of the pile). Then click on the turntable. Experiment with the "Flash" button and microphone to create an all-round studio effect.

 www.playmusic.org

SPIN THE DECKS

Crank up the volume with what must be top of the cyber charts – the **Scratch Simulator**. This great site lets you really play at being a DJ. You can take control of the music with three turntables, strobes, and mikes, which let you make your own mix of the records and sounds. Just click your mouse around and see what you can come up with. Play with the lighting – look out for the bare bulbs. Try all three levels, red, yellow, and blue, and get those dancing shoes really moving!

 www.turntables.de/scratchit8.htm

TUNE IN

There are plenty of sites that give you access to free MP3 players, but also check out the virtual radio station and music searcher, **RadioSpy**. Tune in to find all the best digital broadcasts and music files on the web. Music to your ears!

 www.radiospy.com

TOP TIP
An MP3 is a compressed music file. This means that your computer has less information to read before it can play the track, but it still sounds as good as a CD. For more info visit: www.MP3.com

SPORTING CHANCE

You might not think the web has much to offer a sports fanatic. But on days when it's too hot, too cold, or too wet to play, you can indulge your sports cravings by surfing the tens of thousands of sports sites. They offer fanzines, news servers, fantasy leagues, and all the sports facts. What gives online sports its edge is that it is all day, every day, so on your marks...get set...go!

This site's attractions include its own magazine, kid polls, and forums, and a whole set of fantasy sports leagues.

www.sikids.com

TITLE CONTENDERS

If you're truly on the ball, then the place to be for a great general sports site is **Sports Illustrated For Kids**. The "Shorter reporter" provides all the latest news and reviews on almost any sport. There's also a trivia challenge, a "Laugh locker" with sports gags, and a "Sports arcade" where you can test your own game skills.

GO FOR GOLD

Click on "Kids" and explore the zones. Check out "Olly's joke jam" in the "Worldzone."

For a medal-winning website, visit **Olympics.com**. There's info on all olympic sports and the world's top stars, as well as news and previews from Sydney and Athens 2004.

www.olympics.com/eng

At The Locker Room you can get expert tips for improving your own sports skills.

SPORTS SKILLS

The Locker Room is the perfect place to find out about your favorite sport. It carries bios of sports legends, explains rules, offers good advice on equipment, and comes fully loaded with fascinating facts.

 http://members.aol.com/msdaizy/sports/locker.html

WEB WATCH

Find even more sports info at **Sky Sports.** It features updated news flashes and articles on every sport in the book. With expert columns, interviews with the stars, listings, and superb action photos, this is one stop you can't afford to miss.
www.sky.com/sports

🔺🔺🏴 ⚡⚡⚡ www.football365.co.uk

⬇ TOUCHDOWN

For football fans, the place to get physical is **Play Football**, the NFL's official kids' site. Try out "NFL Flag," a great game for kids who want to find out more about the game and develop their football skills. Click on "Get involved," and check out "Punt, pass and kick" and the junior NFL league. You can also take a look at the video highlights of past games.

🕷 🕷 🕷 🕷

> This NFL site offers lots of news and reviews, polls, video highlights, football facts, and the chance to go behind the scenes to find out what life is like for the referee!

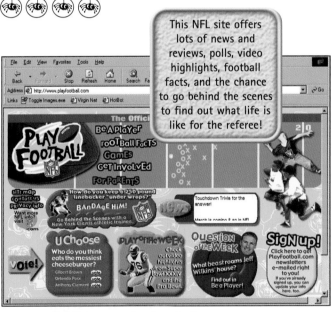

🔺🔺🏴⚡⚡⚡www.playfootball.com

◀ BACK OF THE NET

Soccer fans who want to get a good overall picture of the world of soccer should visit the **Football 365** site. It's got all the latest news, expert features, and fixture previews, as well as its own e-zine, and fun interactive stuff too. For the hardened armchair athlete, tune in to the live score updates, discussion forums, and commentary.

🕷 🕷 🕷

🔺🔺 ⚡⚡⚡⚡ www.fastball.com/playball

🔺 FIRST BASE

There is a lot of baseball info on the internet with sites like **Fastball.com** offering lightning news flashes, "Dugout chat," and some amazing Ipix visuals with Omniview. 🕷 🕷 🕷

> To improve your own tennis, you can find out how the stars train and prepare for matches with the top tips archive.

🔺🔺🏴 ⚡⚡⚡ www.tennis.com

🔺 AN ACE SITE!

For faultless service go to **Tennis.com**. All the latest news, some great top player profiles, and links to all the stars' websites. 🕷 🕷 🕷

ADVENTURE OF A LIFETIME

For the ultimate sports buzz, step forward and enter the world of the extreme. This is not for the fainthearted, so if you think tiddlywinks is quite a thrill, then you should probably stay at home. If not, get your ticket here at **Adventure Living** and find out about adventure sports, coping with extreme climates, and physical endurance. Read amazing stories of real-life experiences of danger and adventure in the mountains, skies, and seas.

Under "Adventures," choose between white-water rafting, skydiving, and SCUBA diving.

Click on "Slide show" and sit back and enjoy the pictures. They load automatically.

🎖🎖 ⚡⚡⚡ www.adventureliving.com

🎖🎖 ⚡⚡⚡ http://library.thinkquest.org/28170

GOING FOR SNOW

This is another **ThinkQuest** site that gives you all the history and facts about snowboarding. There are great photos and interviews, as well as all the lingo you'll need out on the slopes. Find out why you might be "goofy," and learn what "carving" is all about.

TAKE THE PLUNGE

This is a great **ThinkQuest** site that takes you to SCUBA school to learn all about diving. Find out exactly what the risks are, and learn about the techniques and methods of protection used to make it safer. Test your knowledge with the quiz and message board, and look through the "Biographies" (under "History and development") of inspirational divers of the past. The only thing, of course, is that there's no guarantee about what, or who, you might find down there!

Try the "Diving quiz" under "Diving inter@ctive."

🎖🎖 ⚡⚡⚡ http://tqjunior.advanced.org/3885

▶ YO-YO MAD!

You've hung out with the stars and been to the edge and back with the extremists, but what about the weird and quirky? This is a website dedicated to yo-yos, and if you think yo-yos are just kids' toys, then think again. Enroll at the "Yomega University of Yo-yos" and find out what tricks you've got up your sleeve.

WEB WATCH

For some frisbee fun, visit **Freestyle Frisbee** and impress your friends at the beach with a "Pancake" catch or a "Between the legs" throw. There are frisbee-handling tips for all levels.
www.frisbee.com

Learn yo-yo moves such as "Popping the clutch," the "Spaghetti," and the "Eiffel Tower." Join the "Yomega Yo-Yo Association," take the advanced quiz, and learn how to do the "Trick of the month."

🪂🪂🪂 ⚡⚡⚡ www.yomega.com

Animated lessons teach you how to juggle with three and four balls.

🪂🪂✈ ⚡⚡⚡
http://home.eznet.net/~stevemd

⏺ WHAT GOES UP...

... must come down. Learn how to juggle at **This + That**. It's the perfect place to find out what a pair of hands can do. Read the top entertainers' tips, and prepare to wow your friends. And remember, keep your eye on the balls – all of them!

There are tons of tips and animated activities. Learn all you can, then see if you can put your expertise into practice on the sports field.

🪂🪂🪂 ⚡⚡⚡⚡ www.exploratorium.edu

⏺ SPORTS SCIENCE

This **Exploratorium** website takes you through the whys and wherefores of sport. Click on "Sport! Science" and choose a sport. You can find out why balls bounce and how to put a curve on a baseball throw. 🕷🕷🕷🕷

TOP TIP
Ever wanted to be a sports coach? Try: www.fantasysportshq.com For soccer, head for: www.fantasyleague.com

ANIMAL KINGDOM

You don't need to go to Africa to see big cats, or to Florida to spot an alligator; the animal kingdom is alive and well on the internet, and seeing exotic animals only takes a few clicks of your mouse. There's something for everyone, whether it's pet portraits, the food chain, snakes, or facts about evolution that you're after. Let your mouse lead the way, and get online for some real internet animal magic!

WILD WORLD

To understand the entire animal food chain, from the tropics to the arctic, there's only one place to go - the **World Wildlife Fund** homepage. Click on the "Kids" tab and choose from the many games, factsheets, quizzes, and activities. In the "Virtual house," enter rooms to find out about endangered animals, threats to the environment, and biodiversity. The "Pennies for the Planet" newsletter gives you all the news from the animal world.

www.worldwildlife.org

ANIMAL ACTION

If you've already visited the World Wildlife Fund site then you'll know that many of the world's most exotic and exciting animals are in serious danger. So wander around **Kids' Planet** and find out what you can do to help save endangered species such as the rhino and the shy giant panda.

Find out which animals are in danger where with the "Color your world" map.

DEFEND IT!

There are tips on supporting wildlife, as well as facts, games, and quizzes.

Go to "Wild games" to try the "Who am I?" noises test.

www.kidsplanet.org

File Edit View Favorites Tools Help

Back Forward Stop Refresh Home Search Favorites History Mail Print

Address http://www.pbs.org/lifeofbirds/ Go

Links Toggle Images.exe Virgin Net HotBot

PBS Home Search Programs A-Z TV Schedules Shop Station Finder

Click on "Evolution" to see birds that lived 150 million years ago.

Listen to the "Bird songs" of the kakapo bird.

 www.pbs.org/lifeofbirds

🔻 COOL FOR CATS

Visit **Big Cats Online** and you'll never look at your pet tabby in the same way again. It features weird and wacky facts about your cat's distant cousins and wild relatives. Find out the difference between the lone predator and domestic cat and discover how they get their names. There is definitely more to these mysterious creatures than meets the eye.

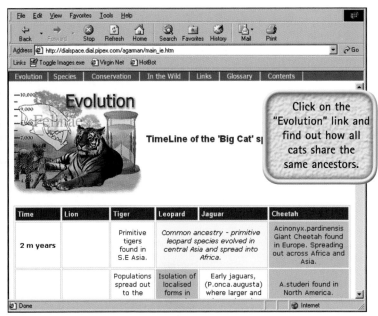

File Edit View Favorites Tools Help

Back Forward Stop Refresh Home Search Favorites History Mail Print

Address http://dialspace.dial.pipex.com/agarman/main_ie.htm Go

Links Toggle Images.exe Virgin Net HotBot

Evolution Species Conservation In the Wild Links Glossary Contents

Evolution

TimeLine of the 'Big Cat' s[...]

Click on the "Evolution" link and find out how all cats share the same ancestors.

Time	Lion	Tiger	Leopard	Jaguar	Cheetah
2 m years		Primitive tigers found in S.E Asia.	Common ancestry - primitive leopard species evolved in central Asia and spread into Africa.		Acinonyx.pardinensis Giant Cheetah found in Europe. Spreading out across Africa and Asia.
		Populations spread out to the	Isolation of localised forms in	Early jaguars, (P.onca.augusta) where larger and	A.studeri found in North America.

Done Internet

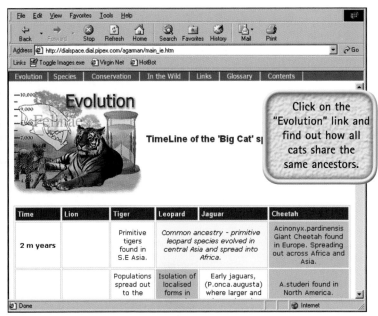 www.dialspace.dial.pipex.com/agarman

🔵 BIRD BRAINS

You might not pay much attention to birds, but visit the PBS **The Life of Birds** site, and you'll soon take notice. Check out the humming bird that flaps its wings up to 1,000 times a second, or the cunning crow that gets us to prepare dinner for it.

🔻 PET PICTURES

You'll find **The Pet Channe**l caters to most pets. Head for the "Funstuff" and check out the daily cartoons, and then go to "Kids corner." Send in a picture of your own pet and see if it's picked as "Pet of the day" in the photo gallery.

 www.thepetchannel.com

 http://lam.vet.uga.edu/kids

🔺 HORSING AROUND

Learn to be a junior vet with this interactive site. Ask questions and get answers from a real vet, try the games, and enter competitions.

▶ SOMETHING FISHY

Witness a biting encounter at Discovery Online's **Shark Tank.** Download the Ipix plug-in, and you can watch sharks go through their paces in 3-D. Click on any of the sharks in the tank and read its personal profile – get acquainted with the Goblin, Hammer, Great White, and Spiny Dogfish.

View the shark tank through a "PhotoBubble" and get a 360° view as you swim with the sharks.

SHARK Tank

More than 350 different kinds of sharks patrol our waters. We've gathered a few of them together in our shark tank, so dive in and explore.

TODAY AT THE SHARK LAB

TRACK OUR PROGRESS

www.discovery.com/stories/nature/sharkweek/tank.html

Click on the "Voyage to the deep" tab and join the crew in a deep-sea submarine called "Alvin."

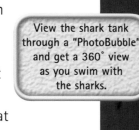

www.ocean.udel.edu/deepsea/level-1/creature/creature.html

▶ FANGS A MILLION!

Slither along to **The Snake.org** and come eye to eye with pythons, vipers, and boas. Check out the sections on "Snake bites" and the world's "Deadliest snakes."

www.thesnake.org

● ROCK BOTTOM

Travel to the bottom of the ocean with **Voyage to the Deep.** Reach depths of almost two miles, where there is no natural light, or dare to click on Creature Feature's "Denizens of the deep" and plug into a video of a deep-sea octopus!

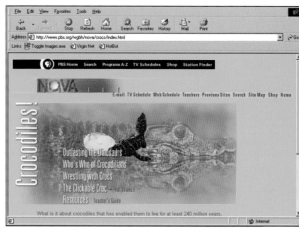

www.pbs.org/wgbh/nova/crocs/index.html

▲ CROC CRAZY

Use "The clickable croc" at this **Crocodiles!** site to find out what makes crocodiles tick. They won't use their teeth to chew you – they prefer to swallow their prey whole!

www.EnchantedLearning.com/subjects/sharks/index.htm ...and, /whales/index.html

▶ TO THE MAX!

Anyone who thought dinosaurs were extinct is in for a big shock! What better place to see the dinosaur revival than **Imax**, the site where great links and amazing graphics bring T-rex back from the grave.

> See what "Ally Hayden" has to say about life as a self-confessed dino-freak.

> "Visit the Cretaceous Period" and try a zoom lens that lets you get up close to the dinosaurs.

> Download a scary T-rex screensaver.

🚂🚂 ⚡⚡⚡⚡ www.imax.com/t-rex

⬤ WALK ON THE WILD SIDE

For those with nerves of steel, try the BBC **Walking with Dinosaurs** site. Travel back to the late Triassic period on an interactive journey where you decide when and where to stop.

🚂🚂 ⚡⚡⚡⚡ www.bbc.co.uk/dinosaurs

> Jump to "Dinosaur worlds" and hear a T-rex roar, or get a pterosaur eye view of the world.

⬤ DINO MOVES

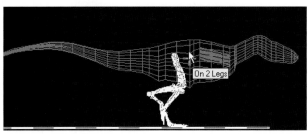

Discovery Online's **Fossil Zone** features some really hi-tech animation. "Look at dino motion" and click on the cursor to make the T-rex move. Don't forget to visit the "Gallery of the strange."

🚂🚂 ⚡⚡⚡⚡ www.discovery.com/exp/fossilzone/fossilzone.html

WEB CRAWLERS

Insects are everywhere, not least on the worldwide web. To find out about the insect world, you don't have to get your hands dirty, just follow our guide to those websites dedicated to all things that wriggle, slither, and buzz in the night...

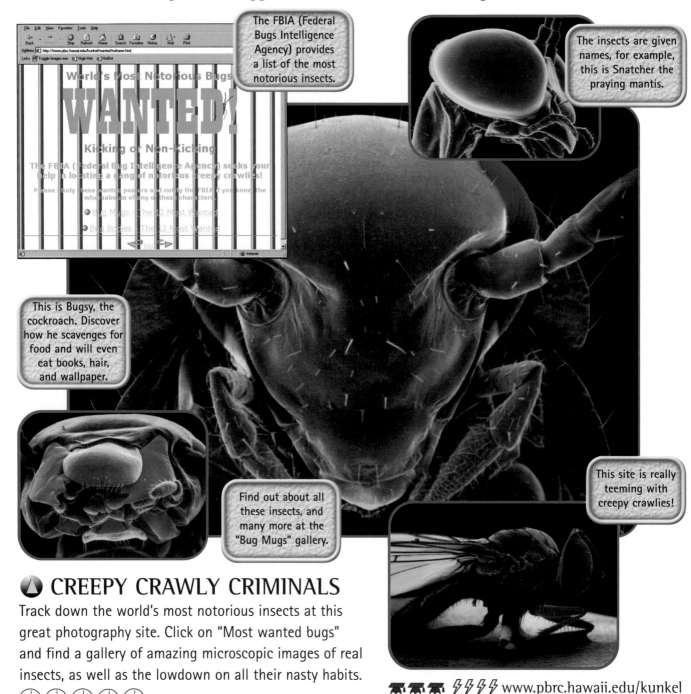

The FBIA (Federal Bugs Intelligence Agency) provides a list of the most notorious insects.

The insects are given names, for example, this is Snatcher the praying mantis.

This is Bugsy, the cockroach. Discover how he scavenges for food and will even eat books, hair, and wallpaper.

This site is really teeming with creepy crawlies!

Find out about all these insects, and many more at the "Bug Mugs" gallery.

CREEPY CRAWLY CRIMINALS

Track down the world's most notorious insects at this great photography site. Click on "Most wanted bugs" and find a gallery of amazing microscopic images of real insects, as well as the lowdown on all their nasty habits.

www.pbrc.hawaii.edu/kunkel

▶ IT'S A BUG'S LIFE

Learn all the basics about insects on the **Bug Page** by clicking on "Insect tutorial." In the "Entomology forum" you can ask questions and chat with fellow bug enthusiasts. There is also a picture gallery where you can check the names of insects you may have seen out and about. Also click onto one of the dozens of links to other great insect sites on the web.

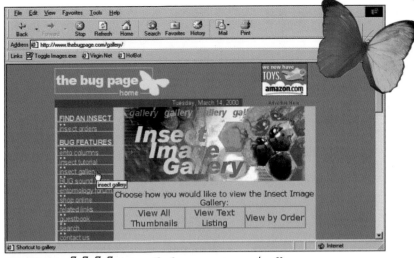

🦋🦋🦋 ⚡⚡⚡⚡ www.thebugpage.com/gallery

> Herman tells you his life story, many facts about worms, and all about his insect friends who live nearby.

🦋🦋🦋 ⚡⚡⚡⚡ www.urbanext.uiuc.edu/kids/index.html

◀ WORM SITE

Join in the fun and games with Herman the worm on a lively journey through his world. Not only will you discover all about worms, but you'll also meet Herman's friends Mickey Mite and Milly Millipede.

▶ GROSS ROACH

Join Ralph Roach at **Yucky's Bug World** for insights into how insect pests behave. Ralph Roach even lets you read his diary, describing a day in his life and letting you in on his eating habits and favorite hiding places.

🦋🦋🦋 ⚡⚡⚡

www.yucky.com/roaches

▶ EYE SPY

Insects might not win many beauty contests, but you should see what we look like to them! **B-Eye** lets you look through the eyes of a bee. Can you guess who this is?

🦋🦋🦋 ⚡⚡⚡

http://cvs.anu.edu.au/andy/beye

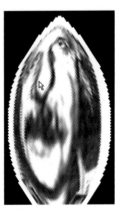

TIME TRAVEL

A journey through time may not be possible yet, but you can get pretty close by surfing the web. Turn back the clock and visit ancient Rome, take part in the original Olympic Games in Athens, or book your ticket on a Mayan adventure.

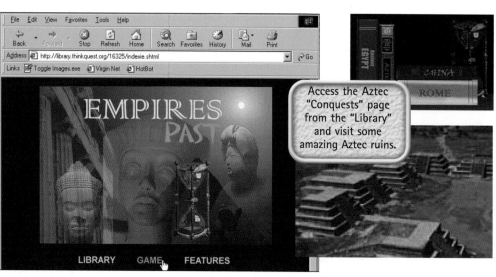

Access the Aztec "Conquests" page from the "Library" and visit some amazing Aztec ruins.

WAK-A-GLADIATOR

🔺🔺🔺 ⚡⚡⚡⚡ http://library.thinkquest.org/16325/feat.html

🔺 THE EMPIRE STRIKES BACK

This great **ThinkQuest** site lets you visit the mighty empires of ancient Rome, China, Egypt, and the Aztecs, with great visuals, videos, and games.

🕷️🕷️🕷️🕷️🕷️

Go to the "Game" section and challenge a gladiator.

🔺 MAYAN MAPS

Don't get lost! Here's a map to let you take in all the sights on a Mayan adventure, from the Temple of Tikal to the monuments of Uxmal. Take a look at the "Maya photo archive" – truly spectacular! 🕷️🕷️🕷️

🔺🔺🔺 ⚡⚡⚡⚡ www.smm.org/sln/ma

WEB WATCH
For great time-travel tourism, check out the guide to **The Seven Wonders of the Ancient World.** From the statue of Zeus at Olympia to the Hanging Gardens of Babylon, they put modern buildings to shame! http://ce.eng.usf.edu/pharos/wonders/

WHEN IN ROME

Latin might be a dead language, but with the **Forum Romanum** site you can see Julius Caesar's world brought back to life. Take a virtual tour behind the scenes and even learn a bit of the lingo.

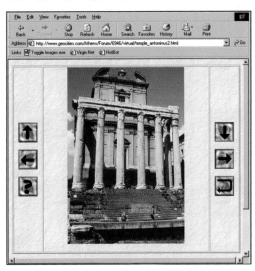

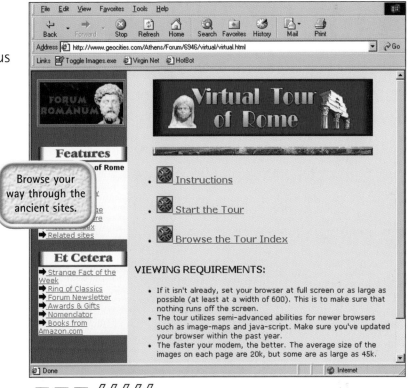

Browse your way through the ancient sites.

www.geocities.com/Athens/Forum/6946/virtual/virtual.html

THE KINGDOM OF THE NILE

Go even further back, and call in on the mummies at the "Mysteries of Egypt" in this virtual museum. Take the "Elevator" to "Level 3," and get your ticket at the "Civilizations Hall." Then set off on the virtual tour of Tutankhamun's tomb.

WEB WATCH
Learn how to write like the Egyptians at the "Online hieroglyphic translator":
www.quizland.com/hiero.htm

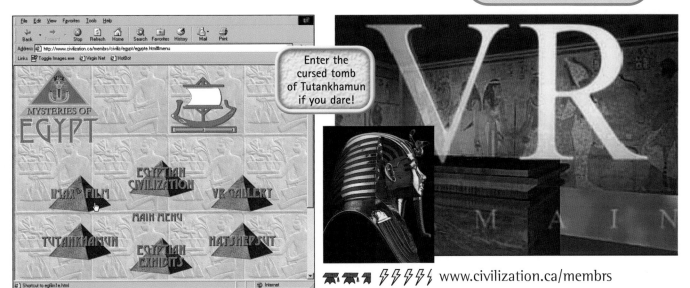

Enter the cursed tomb of Tutankhamun if you dare!

www.civilization.ca/membrs

YOUR HISTORY

Whether you're fed up with trying to remember the date of the Battle of Hastings, the name of Henry VIII's fourth wife, or what the Gettysburg Address was all about, help is at hand; the web has lots of interesting ways of making history come to life. Solve historical mysteries, take a tour around the White House as it was a hundred years ago, and find out whether you're related to Napoleon. There's no doubt about it, with sites like these, history's got a great future.

▶ BACK IN TIME

There are buckets of great history sites out there if it's just information that you want. But the **Hyper History Online** directory, with snazzy links to some great sites, makes most look prehistoric. Pick a person, event, or time, and you're on your way.

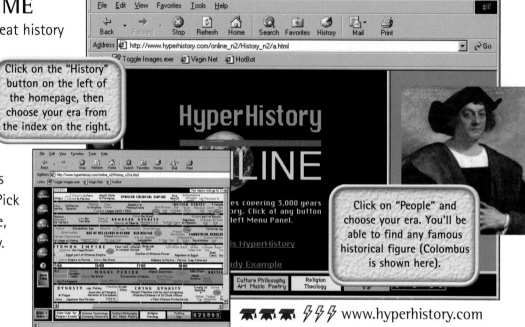

> Click on the "History" button on the left of the homepage, then choose your era from the index on the right.

> Click on "People" and choose your era. You'll be able to find any famous historical figure (Colombus is shown here).

🦅🦅🦅 ⚡⚡⚡ www.hyperhistory.com

Messengers of Light

> Find out about Joan of Arc, Genghis Khan, and many more historical figures.

 ⚡⚡⚡ www.sangha.net/messengers/all-pantheon.htm

◀ WHO'S WHO

It might be more of a Hall of Shame than a Hall of Fame, but history is full of some pretty colorful characters. For a selective list, click on the **Pantheon of the Great Brotherhood of Light**. It's big on saints and prophets, but it also has great stuff on some of the nastier individuals they fought against! There are fantastic pictures, and you should be able to get help for any school history projects you are tackling as well.

🦅🦅🦅🦅

Welcome to the
WorldRoots
Genealogy Archive

 www.worldroots.com

TREE CLIMBING

You know that famous historical figures are interesting, but what about your own family? If you're convinced you're related to royalty, check out this **World Roots** site. Click on the "Site map" and have a good look around. The author has spent a long time proving her family connections – use her expertise to find out yours. She traces her family back to German princes and princesses, so you never know, you could be next in line for the throne without even knowing it!

GREAT INVENTIONS

Click on "The lab" on this great **CBC4kids** website and check out the "History of inventions." Things you take for granted all had to be invented at some point, and this webpage features anything from the wheel to traffic lights and hot dogs.

Take a closer look at this early bike.

www.cbc4kids.ca

TOP TIP
If all this talk of families has given you the genealogy bug, there are lots of ways to chart your own family tree online. Try:
www.Myfamily.com

VIRTUAL WHITE HOUSE

Get an inside view of what the White House looked like 100 years ago. Click on "White House history and tours" on the homepage and have a good look around.

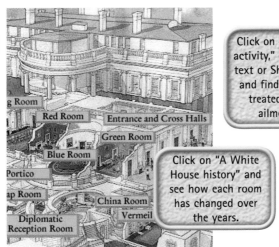

Red Room
Entrance and Cross Halls
Green Room
Blue Room
Portico
China Room
Vermeil
Diplomatic Reception Room

Click on "A White House history" and see how each room has changed over the years.

www.whitehouse.gov

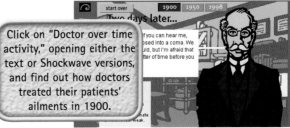

Click on "Doctor over time activity," opening either the text or Shockwave versions, and find out how doctors treated their patients' ailments in 1900.

start over   1900 1950 1998
Two days later...

www.pbs.org/wgbh/aso/tryit/doctor

MEDICAL HISTORY

Visit the Victorian doctor at the **Science Odyssey**. With medicine like this, you would never be sick again!

PICTURE THIS

Ever heard the expression, "a picture is worth a thousand words"? Well, there's no better place to find out how true that is than the internet. There are dozens of amazing sites taking you through the history of the greatest works of art ever created, with virtual tours, and even the chance for you to create your own masterpieces.

▶ IN THE FRAME

Brush up at the **Web Gallery**, and trace the history of art from the early Renaissance (the 14th century) to 1750. Check out the "Glossary" for explanations of the different schools of art and artistic techniques, and if you click on the alphabetical listing you'll get information about every artist and painting in the book. It's pretty as a picture!

> Click on "Chef d'oeuvre" (that's "masterpiece" in French). There is an audio commentary and five tours of top modern artists in the "Virtual gallery."

> Click on "Tours" and take tour 5 for this view of the ceiling of the Sistine Chapel. It's very high up so you might want to use the zoom tool to examine the best parts.

25% 50% 75% 100% 150% 200% Fit width Fit height

> You can send webcards of your favorite paintings to your friends.

🎭🎭🎭 ⚡⚡⚡⚡⚡ www.kfki.hu/~arthp/index1.html

◀ FIRST IMPRESSION

If it's Monet, Dali, and Picasso you're after, then stop by for a private viewing and explanations by experts. **Modern Masterworks.**

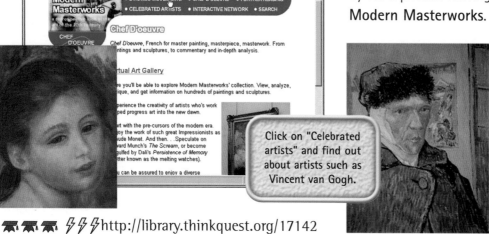

Back Forward Stop Refresh Home Search Favorites History Mail Print
Address http://library.thinkquest.org/17142/chef-doeuvre/index.htm Go
Links Toggle Images.exe Virgin Net HotBot

Modern Masterworks
● DYNAMIC MOVEMENTS ● CHEF D'OEUVRE ● FURTHER READING
● CELEBRATED ARTISTS ● INTERACTIVE NETWORK ● SEARCH

CHEF D'OEUVRE

Chef D'oeuvre

Chef D'oeuvre, French for master painting, masterpiece, masterwork. From ...ntings and sculptures, to commentary and in-depth analysis.

...rtual Art Gallery

...re you'll be able to explore Modern Masterworks' collection. View, analyze, ...ique, and get information on hundreds of paintings and sculptures.

...perience the creativity of artists who's work ...ped progress art into the new dawn.

...art with the pre-cursors of the modern era. ...joy the work of such great Impressionists as ...ude Monet. And then. . .Speculate on ...ard Munch's *The Scream*, or become ...gulfed by Dali's *Persistence of Memory* ...tter known as the melting watches).

...u can be assured to enjoy a diverse

> Click on "Celebrated artists" and find out about artists such as Vincent van Gogh.

🎭🎭🎭 ⚡⚡⚡ http://library.thinkquest.org/17142

WEB WATCH
What do you know about art? Test yourself at:
http://library.thinkquest.org/17142/interactivenetwork/modern-art-101.htm

▶ CARTOON CAPERS

Art doesn't just mean the Renaissance or the Impressionists. Go down to **Cartoon World** for some moving pictures and meet up with the toon folks. On the homepage there is a menu of different types of cartoons. Take your pick from "Action," "Adventure," and "Mystery," or go galactic at "Starblazers."

Get involved at "Fun and games," with interactive puzzles and cartoon coloring sheets.

www.cet.com/~rascal/welcome.html

▼ CLOWNING AROUND

For more hands-on artistry, take your brush and palette over to the **nfx Cartoon-O-Matic**. Take control of the nfx distorter, and change cartoon faces by morphing the shape and size of their noses, ears, eyes, and mouths. You can choose which characters you think could do with a facelift on the homepage.

Change the faces of a variety of cartoon characters. Click on the one you want to change and then "Go!."

www.nfx.com/cgi-bin/livingart

Follow the instructions to build up Kat's face.

www.abctooncenter.com/kattoon.htm

◀ ART CLASS

Cartoon with Kat by putting his face together, bit by bit, until you get the entire Kat cartoon seen here. Then color him in and you're a cartoonist!

▶ BRING THE HOUSE DOWN

If you want to keep things concrete, then take a look at this really great **ThinkQuest** site, tracing the history of architecture, from ancient to modern.

Click on "Photo album" to see these pics, and many more.

Pyramids of Giza – ancient

Notre Dame Cathedral – gothic

Empire State Building – modern

http://tqjunior.advanced.org/3786

VIRTUAL GLOBETROTTER

There's no need to take long-haul flights or seasick boat trips to travel the world; you can reach all destinations via the web. There are some amazing sites online, with great views, natural features, city scenes, and extraordinary wildlife from all over the globe.

Check out web cams and videos of places from the Arctic to the tropics. There's also a great film clip of a Madagascan chameleon catching its prey.

www.sci.mus.mn.us/greatestplaces

THE TRAVEL BUG

From east to west, **The Greatest Places Online** brings you global highlights that will give you a taste for traveling. You can discover the nomads of Tibet or watch a video of Amazonian wildlife.

Visit "Greenland" for a Quicktime 360˚ tour of the "Space huts." Use the cursor keys to move around and the magnifying glass icon to zoom in and out.

Scroll through the site directory, and take in an "Africam" Safari or Niagara Falls.

www.earthcamforkids.com

THE WORLD IN ACTION

Visit many of the world's most stunning landmarks with **EarthCam for Kids**. This is the top cam search engine, where you can click on subjects from adventure parks to space, and be taken to some of the best live and archive cam websites online. Attention animal-lovers! There are lots of unusual wildlife shots.

www.ag.net

Check out the Sky Eye Photo Gallery to view some of the world's greatest mountains.

www.sannichi-ybs.co.jp/YBS/SKYEYE/GALLERY/index.html

▶ TAKE A WORLD TOUR

It's fascinating to see how people live around the world. To meet the children living in the Amazon rain forest and get an insight into their daily lives, visit **Let's Go Around the World**. To find out more about a particular scene or animal, simply click on "Tell me about it."

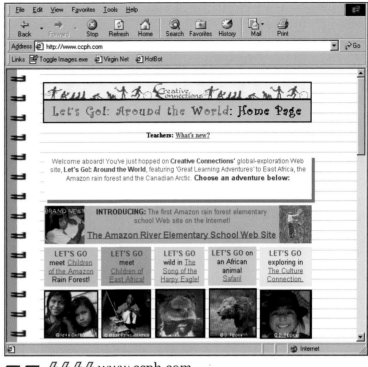

Meet children from a school in the heart of the rain forest, and see what inspires their artistic creations.

🦇🦇 ⚡⚡⚡⚡ www.ccph.com

◑ USING MAPS

If you're inspired to visit someplace, then you'll need a map so you don't get lost. Go to **MapQuest** and you can call up city maps from across the globe. The site is interactive, and you can zoom in on the area you're interested in.

If you're a city dweller, zoom in close and you might find your own street!

🦇🦇 ⚡⚡⚡⚡ www.mapquest.com

WEB WATCH

Once you've caught the traveling bug, you'll want to communicate with people who speak different languages. Take a quick trip to the **Little Explorers** site and learn Spanish, French, and Portuguese with the help of picture dictionaries. **www.EnchantedLearning.com/Dictionary.html**

TOP TIP
The National Geographic Map Machine site has lots of different types of maps and a guide to the world's national flags. www.nationalgeographic.com/maps/index.html

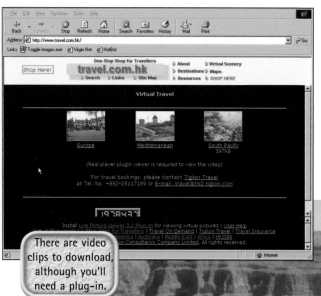

PERFECT POSTCARDS

For an impressive travel album, visit **Travel.com**'s "Virtual scenery" pages and print out some of their great postcard pictures. The most famous tourist hot spots are there to help you build an inspiring collection of pictures, including the Eiffel Tower in Paris, the pyramids of Egypt, and Manhattan's Statue of Liberty.

> There are video clips to download, although you'll need a plug-in.

www.travel.com.hk/gallery

> Search by location. Choose between Africa, Asia, Europe, America, the Middle East, and Australia.

Bear in Brazil

Nile River, Egypt

Lismore, Australia

Hiddensee Island, Germany

Machu Picchu, Peru

Buenos Aires, Argentina

Santiago, Chile Anti-Pinochet rally 1990

Berlin, Germany

Mt Sinai, Egypt

Dome of Rock, Jerusalem

> Click on "Urban EXcentrics," then "Musical world tour" for a soundtrack to go with the pictures.

> See pictures of the Berlin Wall, Machu Picchu, or the city of Cairo.

GLOBAL GALLERY

However long your vacation, whether it's two weeks in the country or a weekend in the big city, it seems you can never fit everything in. But, with the **Urban EXcentrics World Tour**, you can be sure that you won't miss anything. A funky soundtrack keeps you entertained while you take in global highlights across all five continents. It points the camera at the most weird and wonderful sights the world has to offer, as well as giving good advice for travelers (click on "Travel tips").

www.iinet.net.au/~property/travel_index.html

◗ CYBER ACTION

Vacations aren't only about lying on a beach. Get active at **Adventure Online** and join the daring crews on their real-life adventures. You can follow intrepid explorers every step of the way, reading their travel log and seeing all the amazing sights. Whether you like cycling through Africa, or kayaking along the crocodile-infested Nile, someone at Adventure Online will be doing it and will invite you along, via the internet, for the adventure of a lifetime.

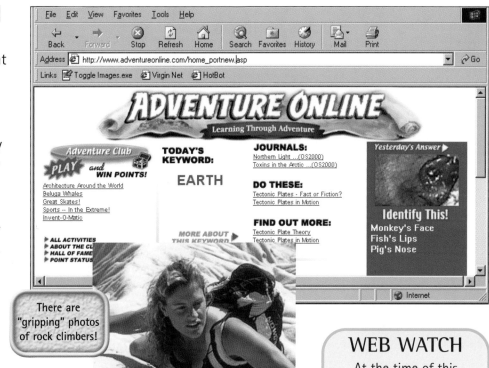

File   Edit   View   Favorites   Tools   Help

Back   Forward   Stop   Refresh   Home   Search   Favorites   History   Mail   Print

Address http://www.adventureonline.com/home_portnew.asp   Go

Links   Toggle Images.exe   Virgin Net   HotBot

ADVENTURE ONLINE
Learning Through Adventure

Adventure Club
PLAY and WIN POINTS!

Architecture Around the World
Beluga Whales
Great Skates!
Sports -- In the Extreme!
Invent-O-Matic

▶ ALL ACTIVITIES
▶ ABOUT THE CLUB
▶ HALL OF FAME
▶ POINT STATUS

TODAY'S KEYWORD:

EARTH

MORE ABOUT THIS KEYWORD ▶

JOURNALS:
Northern Light ...(OS2000)
Toxins in the Arctic ...(OS2000)

DO THESE:
Tectonic Plates - Fact or Fiction?
Tectonic Plates in Motion

FIND OUT MORE:
Tectonic Plate Theory
Tectonic Plates in Motion

Yesterday's Answer ▶

Identify This!
Monkey's Face
Fish's Lips
Pig's Nose

Internet

There are "gripping" photos of rock climbers!

www.adventureonline.com

Meet Buzz Kaplan and his crew at base camp just before they embark on a transcontinental flight from the Caribbean, across South America, all the way to Antarctica.

WEB WATCH

At the time of this writing, the **Adventure Online** team is developing a section just for kids. It's due out in Fall 2000 and looks pretty good so far. It will have four categories: "Expeditions," "Camping," "Animals," and "Sports"; so watch out for it!

In the tropics you'll find more plants and wildlife than anywhere else on the planet.

Visit the Perito Moreno glacier.

Fly over Buenos Aires at night and see the sights.

WORLD WATCH

The answers to all your questions about the world around us can be found on the web. Take a guided tour around some of the web's top global sites and you can step inside a live volcano, head into a swirling hurricane, or go back to the birth of time. You can even take control of weather systems, move them around, and see what happens...

> Click on "Control the Earth" and get a chance to rule the world! See what happens when you alter the Earth's atmosphere.

> Click on "Through Earth's history" and then "A difficult birth" and take a peek at the Earth's infancy, when comets rained down from the sky.

🐦🐦🐦 ⚡⚡⚡ www.discovery.com

🔺 DOWN TO EARTH

For the first step of the journey, go to **Discovery Online**, and get a taste of life at the eye of the storm. Take control of the Earth's environment and simulate your own weather patterns, or check out natural catastrophes, past and present. Unbeatable! 🕷️🕷️🕷️🕷️🕷️

> Click on "Planet cam" and look through Discovery's live cams to put the whole globe at your fingertips.

> In "Weather" see pictures of "Hurricanes" taken from space.

🐦🐦🐦 ⚡⚡⚡ www.athena.ivv.nasa.gov/index.html

🔺 EARTH SHAKE

Do some global groundwork at **Athena**, "Earth and space science." Look at pictures of storms from space, and learn how to predict the weather. Find out about earthquakes, and check out the section on whales in the "Oceans" category. 🕷️🕷️🕷️

WEB WATCH

Look up these other top websites for some more miscellaneous Earth action:

Tropical forests
www.toucansam.kelloggs.ca
Antarctica
www.pbs.org/wnet/nature/antarctica
The environment
http://tqjunior.thinkquest.org/6076
Maps
www.atlapedia.com
http://cliffie.nosc.mil/~NATLAS

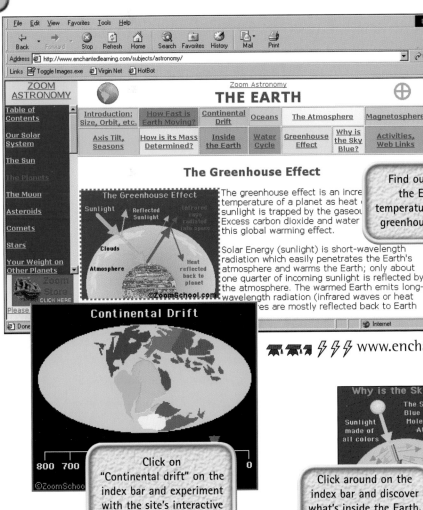

ZOOM ASTRONOMY

THE EARTH

Zoom Astronomy

Table of Contents
Our Solar System
The Sun
The Planets
The Moon
Asteroids
Comets
Stars
Your Weight on Other Planets

Introduction: Size, Orbit, etc. | How Fast is Earth Moving? | Continental Drift | Oceans | The Atmosphere | Magnetosphere
Axis Tilt, Seasons | How is its Mass Determined? | Inside the Earth | Water Cycle | Greenhouse Effect | Why is the Sky Blue? | Activities, Web Links

The Greenhouse Effect

The Greenhouse Effect

Sunlight — Reflected Sunlight — Infrared rays radiated into space
Clouds
Atmosphere
Heat reflected back to planet
©ZoomSchool.com

The greenhouse effect is an increase in temperature of a planet as heat and sunlight is trapped by the gaseous. Excess carbon dioxide and water this global warming effect.

Solar Energy (sunlight) is short-wavelength radiation which easily penetrates the Earth's atmosphere and warms the Earth; only about one quarter of incoming sunlight is reflected by the atmosphere. The warmed Earth emits long-wavelength radiation (infrared waves or heat ... res are mostly reflected back to Earth

Find out about the Earth's temperature and the greenhouse effect.

Continental Drift

800 700 0
©ZoomSchool

Click on "Continental drift" on the index bar and experiment with the site's interactive continental drift program.

CONTINENTAL SURFING

Click on "Earth" on this astronomy homepage, and find out how the continents are slowly shifting on top of a molten sea. Check out the section on "Plate tectonics" (under "Miscellaneous" in the "Table of contents") and see how far the continents have moved in the last 800 million years. In the same section, find out "Why the oceans are salty" and "Why the sky is blue."

www.enchantedlearning.com/subjects/astronomy

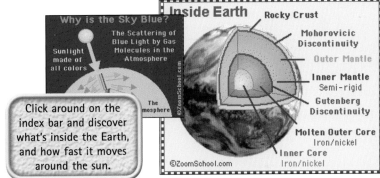

Why is the Sky Blue?

Sunlight made of all colors

The Scattering of Blue Light by Gas Molecules in the Atmosphere
©ZoomSchool.com

Inside Earth

Rocky Crust
Mohorovicic Discontinuity
Outer Mantle
Inner Mantle — Semi-rigid
Gutenberg Discontinuity
Molten Outer Core — Iron/nickel
Inner Core — Iron/nickel
©ZoomSchool.com

Click around on the index bar and discover what's inside the Earth, and how fast it moves around the sun.

EARTH SHAKING

Check out the snazzy activities at **A Science Odyssey**, and download the Shockwave program that lets you play around with tectonic plates. You can cause ocean rifts and mountains to develop. Learn how tectonic plates' movement causes earthquakes and volcanoes in "Intro to plate tectonic theory," and find out where the Earth's longest mountain chain is. A clue: to see it you have to travel downward...

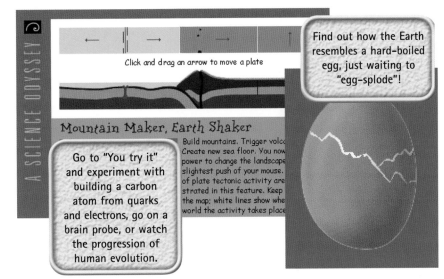

A SCIENCE ODYSSEY

Click and drag an arrow to move a plate

Mountain Maker, Earth Shaker

Build mountains. Trigger volca... Create new sea floor. You now ... power to change the landscape ... slightest push of your mouse. ... of plate tectonic activity are ... strated in this feature. Keep ... the map; white lines show whe... world the activity takes place...

Go to "You try it" and experiment with building a carbon atom from quarks and electrons, go on a brain probe, or watch the progression of human evolution.

Find out how the Earth resembles a hard-boiled egg, just waiting to "egg-splode"!

www.pbs.org/wgbh/aso/tryit/tectonics

▶ HIGH DRAMA

Volcanoes from around the world, particularly those in the United States, feature on the **US Geological Survey (USGS)** site. Click on the volcanoes that interest you for in-depth information and to see a photograph and locator map. You can also marvel at some of the most dramatic eruptions of the 20th century and read about their devastating impact on the places around them.

> You'll find a huge database of facts and photographs at the "Cascades volcano observatory."

http://vulcan.wr.usgs.gov

◀ VOLCANIC VIDEOS

For animated action, join Rocky at **Volcano World**. Click on "Kids' door" for games and puzzles, go on a "Virtual volcano field trip," or zoom in on the "Volcano of the week." You can even find out about extraterrestrial volcanoes like the one on Mars. This site also has a directory of volcanoes, past and present. Best of all, though, are the volcano disaster movies!

> For real-life drama, view movies of lava flow from erupting volcanoes.

> Go to "VW Index," then "Video clips" for films.

http://volcano.und.nodak.edu

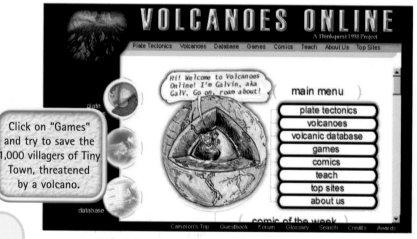

> Click on "Games" and try to save the 1,000 villagers of Tiny Town, threatened by a volcano.

http://library.thinkquest.org/17457

◆ EXPERT GUIDE

Join Galvin at **Volcanoes Online** and he'll explain what causes earthquakes and volcanic eruptions. Click on "The legend" to take a trip back in time to the origins of the term "volcano" in ancient Sicily. The site is interactive so you can click on features you want to know more about.

WEB WATCH

On the web you can discover just how exciting the Earth is – by viewing it from space! Visit **Solarviews.com** for amazing images of Earth, as well as fascinating facts. This site fixes Earth firmly in its place in the cosmos.

www.solarviews.com/eng/earth.htm

UP, UP, AND AWAY

To experience the drama of flying an airplane into the eye of hurricanes and typhoons, join flight navigator **Scott A. Dommin** and his cabin crew in the clouds. Click on "A hurricane hunter's photo album" for amazing close-up photographs taken from inside the storm. You'll also see the lifecycles of hurricanes and typhoons for yourself.

> Find out how search radar enables crews to find the center of hurricanes or typhoons.

 http://members.aol.com/hotelq

STORM BREWING...

The weather forecast will never seem dull again after a visit to the **Miami Science Museum's Hurricane Storm Science** site. Find out how weather patterns form, read stories from hurricane, flood, and earthquake survivors, then take time out for one of the fun meteorological activites. You can find out how to make your own 3-D glasses and then experience the inside of a hurricane in 3-D; or practice being an amateur weather expert with your own homemade weather station.

  www.miamisci.org/hurricane

WEB WEATHER

Take a rain check at the "Hurricanes and cyclones" pages at the **World Book** site. Find out how hurricanes move and what can be done to protect buildings from high winds. They also have lots of weather links as well as great games and project ideas.

 www.worldbook.com/fun/
bth/hurricane/html/hurricane.htm

WEB WATCH

At **Annenberg/CPB Learner.org**, you'll find out how forecasts are made and how rain and snow are formed.
www.learner.org/
exhibits/weather

SPACE

If you've ever dreamed of going to the Moon, or even Mars and Jupiter, join the thousands of people hitching a ride around the cosmos online. A click of the mouse is all it takes to go on a trip that will take you right out beyond the final frontier – and, with a little luck, all the way back again!

Go on a guided tour of an astronaut's wardrobe, and do the interactive "Space activities" in "Space stuff."

http://starchild.gsfc.nasa.gov

STAR TREKKING

For the first leg of your galactic tour, go on the cyber surf of a lifetime courtesy of NASA's **Star Child** site. With different levels to suit all users, this is a great way to go into orbit!

Follow links to "Other good places," including **Amazing Space's** "Hubble deep field academy," where you can train to become an astronaut.

WEB WATCH

For galaxies of stellar information, visit the **Zoom Astronomy** site. Read the cosmic guides, check out the different planets, and take part in astronomy quizzes and puzzles.
www.EnchantedLearning.com/
subjects/astronomy

Click on "Universe," then "Black holes," for this film.

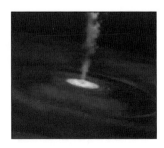

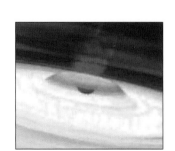

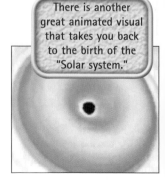

There is another great animated visual that takes you back to the birth of the "Solar system."

1 Travel nearer... 2 ...and nearer... 3 ...to the heart... 4 ...of a black hole!

VOYAGE OF DISCOVERY

For the ultimate high-tech precision images of space, look through the lens of the Hubble Space Telescope at **Discovery.com**. Click on "Hubble's greatest hits" and get coverage of galaxies at the other end of the universe. There are a lot of images and activities that are really quick to load. So if you're looking for an academy to prepare you for a trip to space, enroll here.

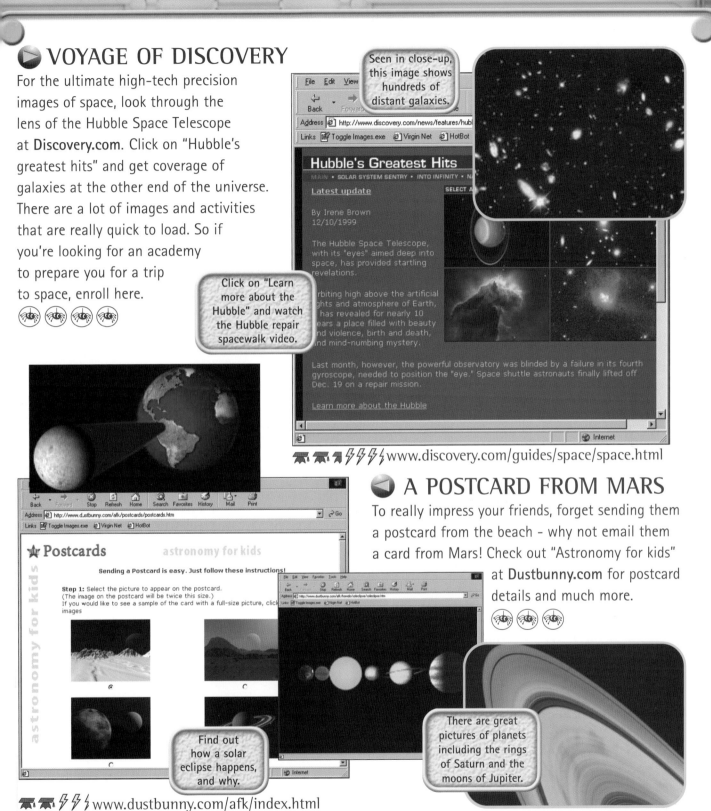

Seen in close-up, this image shows hundreds of distant galaxies.

Click on "Learn more about the Hubble" and watch the Hubble repair spacewalk video.

Hubble's Greatest Hits

MAIN • SOLAR SYSTEM SENTRY • INTO INFINITY • N

Latest update

By Irene Brown
12/10/1999

The Hubble Space Telescope, with its "eyes" aimed deep into space, has provided startling revelations.

Orbiting high above the artificial lights and atmosphere of Earth, it has revealed for nearly 10 years a place filled with beauty and violence, birth and death, and mind-numbing mystery.

Last month, however, the powerful observatory was blinded by a failure in its fourth gyroscope, needed to position the "eye." Space shuttle astronauts finally lifted off Dec. 19 on a repair mission.

Learn more about the Hubble

www.discovery.com/guides/space/space.html

A POSTCARD FROM MARS

To really impress your friends, forget sending them a postcard from the beach - why not email them a card from Mars! Check out "Astronomy for kids" at **Dustbunny.com** for postcard details and much more.

★ **Postcards**   astronomy for kids

Sending a Postcard is easy. Just follow these instructions!

Step 1: Select the picture to appear on the postcard.
(The image on the postcard will be twice this size.)
If you would like to see a sample of the card with a full-size picture, click
images

astronomy for kids

Find out how a solar eclipse happens, and why.

There are great pictures of planets including the rings of Saturn and the moons of Jupiter.

www.dustbunny.com/afk/index.html

WEB WATCH

For a truly interplanetary adventure, take the controls in the cyber cockpit at **A Virtual Journey into the Universe**. Choose a destination and set your speed for hyperspace! **http://library.thinkquest.org/28327**

FUNNY OLD WORLD

Why does a piece of toast always fall jelly-side down? Why don't spiders stick to their own webs? Why do boomerangs come back? And how does a mobile phone work? The world is not a simple place. But don't let it get you down - the answers are out there, and most of them are online.

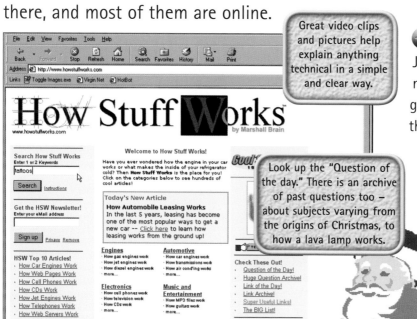

Great video clips and pictures help explain anything technical in a simple and clear way.

Look up the "Question of the day." There is an archive of past questions too – about subjects varying from the origins of Christmas, to how a lava lamp works.

www.howstuffworks.com

QUESTION TIME

Join the quest for the answers to life's mysteries at **How Stuff Works**. If you've got any gadgets at home that need fixing, then look at this site to find out how to go about it. You can learn how almost anything works – remote controls, TVs, the internet, clocks... the list is endless. This is paradise for the curious, with a search engine to find answers to all your questions.

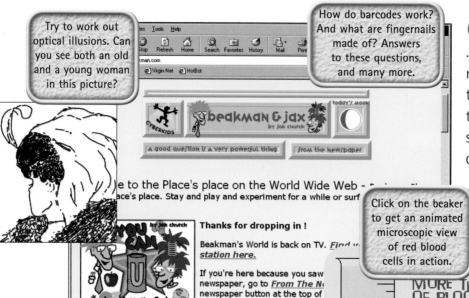

Try to work out optical illusions. Can you see both an old and a young woman in this picture?

How do barcodes work? And what are fingernails made of? Answers to these questions, and many more.

Click on the beaker to get an animated microscopic view of red blood cells in action.

MORE THAN HALF OF BLOOD IS A CLEAR LIQUID !

www.youcan.com

ANYTHING GOES

...with Beakman and Jax. There's no question too weird, nor puzzle too difficult, for them to try to crack. They love the bizarre, so check out their "Most asked questions" and "Interactive demos." You'll be amazed at what you didn't know!

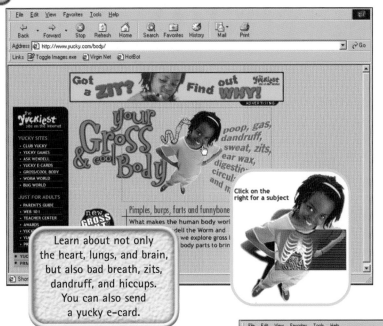

Learn about not only the heart, lungs, and brain, but also bad breath, zits, dandruff, and hiccups. You can also send a yucky e-card.

BODY TALK

You don't have to go very far to find your first mystery. Your own body is a fascinating bag of tricks, and there's no need to ask your doctor to find out something about it. It's much more fun to learn at the **Yucky Gross and Cool Body** site. It features all the things you never knew about how your body works – and probably wished you'd never asked! There are great videos and images to keep it simple, and Wendell the Worm is the perfect host.

www.yucky.com

GOING UP

If you want to earn your wings, head straight for the **K-8 Internet Aeronautical Textbook** and learn how planes stay up in the sky. Click on "Principles of aeronautics" and you can find out about all types of flying machines, from graceful gliders to flying boats, as well as the basic principles of flight.

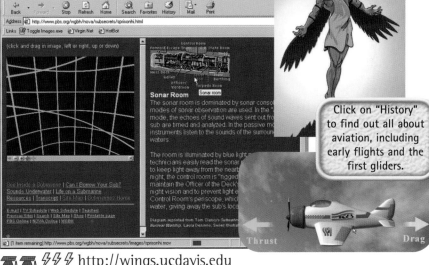

Click on "History" to find out all about aviation, including early flights and the first gliders.

http://wings.ucdavis.edu

Once onboard you can explore the whole ship. Enter the sonar room for a full 3-D submarine experience.

GOING DOWN

There are just as many thrills to be had in the depths of the sea. Take the plunge with **Nova Online**'s **Submarines, Secrets and Spies,** and find out what life is like in a nuclear submarine. Go on virtual tours around USS *Springfield* and USS *Nautilus* (the first nuclear submarine in the world).

www.pbs.org/wgbh/nova/subsecrets

HOMEWORK HELP

If your homework is building up, and relaxing on the couch seems like a distant dream, you can speed things along with some internet research. There is so much information on the web that you can give your work that extra edge to really impress your teachers. From algebra to Shakespeare, you can find what you need. So attack those tricky assignments and make studying fun with the help of these websites.

QUICK ANSWERS

If you want answers at lightning speed then **KidsClick!** could well be the place for you. Like Yahooligans! it searches out information that's just for kids, but with a real study focus. It lets you choose your reading level and decide how much of the web to search. So you just do your own wordsearch, or follow their directory of categories, and you'll soon be surfing the best know-it-all kids' sites available.

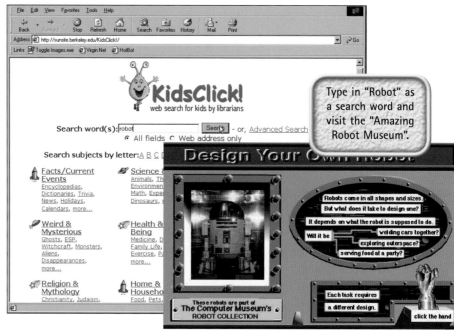

Type in "Robot" as a search word and visit the "Amazing Robot Museum".

http://sunsite.berkeley.edu/KidsClick!

Under "Serious stuff" on the homepage, click on "Homework help" for some excellent study aids.

ONLY THE BEST

If you're ever stuck for a really top-quality site, then **Berit's Best Sites** is the place to go. Stick with the directory, or go for your own wordsearch, and **Berit** will come up with a list of sites. Each site is reviewed, and given a score out of five. What's especially good is that even though they all get a score, it's really selective, so if a site isn't worth visiting, it won't even make the pages of **Berit's** guide.

www.beritsbest.com

WHAT A BONUS!

Have a surf around **Bonus.com**'s **Supersite for Kids.** You'll soon see why it's called a supersite! Your computer has to be able to handle Java, and you may have to download a version of Netscape, but once you're up and running there's no end to the amazing content. You'll find many audio and visual games and puzzles, as well as tons of links to all the facts and figures you could ever need.

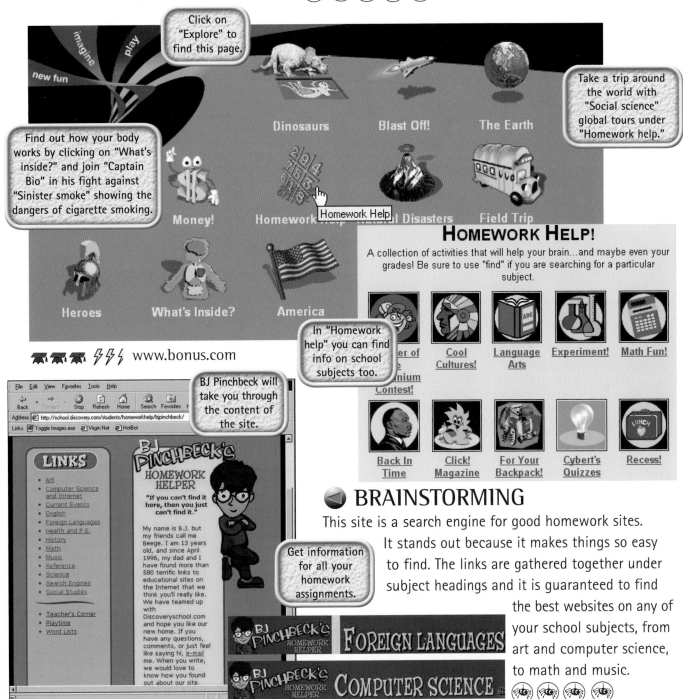

Click on "Explore" to find this page.

Take a trip around the world with "Social science" global tours under "Homework help."

Find out how your body works by clicking on "What's inside?" and join "Captain Bio" in his fight against "Sinister smoke" showing the dangers of cigarette smoking.

Dinosaurs   Blast Off!   The Earth

Money!   Homework Help   Natural Disasters   Field Trip

Heroes   What's Inside?   America

www.bonus.com

In "Homework help" you can find info on school subjects too.

HOMEWORK HELP!

A collection of activities that will help your brain...and maybe even your grades! Be sure to use "find" if you are searching for a particular subject.

...er of ...e ...nium Contest!   Cool Cultures!   Language Arts   Experiment!   Math Fun!

Back In Time   Click! Magazine   For Your Backpack!   Cybert's Quizzes   Recess!

BJ Pinchbeck will take you through the content of the site.

LINKS
- Art
- Computer Science and Internet
- Current Events
- English
- Foreign Languages
- Health and P.E.
- History
- Math
- Music
- Reference
- Science
- Search Engines
- Social Studies

- Teacher's Corner
- Playtime
- Word Lists

BJ PINCHBECK'S HOMEWORK HELPER

"If you can't find it here, then you just can't find it."

My name is B.J. but my friends call me Beege. I am 13 years old, and since April 1996, my dad and I have found more than 580 terrific links to educational sites on the Internet that we think you'll really like. We have teamed up with Discoveryschool.com and hope you like our new home. If you have any questions, comments, or just feel like saying hi, e-mail me. When you write, we would love to know how you found out about our site.

Get information for all your homework assignments.

BJ PINCHBECK'S HOMEWORK HELPER FOREIGN LANGUAGES

BJ PINCHBECK'S HOMEWORK HELPER COMPUTER SCIENCE

www.bjpinchbeck.com

BRAINSTORMING

This site is a search engine for good homework sites. It stands out because it makes things so easy to find. The links are gathered together under subject headings and it is guaranteed to find the best websites on any of your school subjects, from art and computer science, to math and music.

ENCHANTING

Discover the **Enchanted Learning Zoom School** and you'll be able to make your school projects extra special. There are lots of information sheets to print out, as well as quizzes and puzzles to test your knowledge. Find out about the world's most interesting sights and wildlife, and become an expert on dinosaurs, sharks, whales, and other awesome creatures.

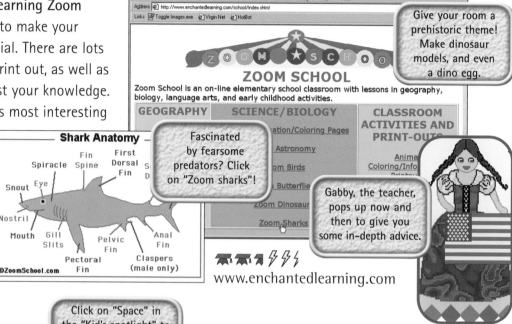

Shark Anatomy

Fin Spine • First Dorsal Fin • Spiracle • Snout • Eye • Nostril • Mouth • Gill Slits • Pectoral Fin • Pelvic Fin • Claspers (male only) • Anal Fin

©ZoomSchool.com

ZOOM SCHOOL

Zoom School is an on-line elementary school classroom with lessons in geography, biology, language arts, and early childhood activities.

| GEOGRAPHY | SCIENCE/BIOLOGY | CLASSROOM ACTIVITIES AND PRINT-OUTS |

> Give your room a prehistoric theme! Make dinosaur models, and even a dino egg.

> Fascinated by fearsome predators? Click on "Zoom sharks"!

> Gabby, the teacher, pops up now and then to give you some in-depth advice.

www.enchantedlearning.com

> Click on "Space" in the "Kid's spotlight" to discover NASA and find out what aeronautical engineers do.

Be a Spacecraft Engineer
STARDUST
Space Junk

...here ... tional Spa ... out the ... Station, it has begun ... Space Station is threatened ... abandoned satellite ... ocket remnants, and many other things.

...ecraft to protect the Space Station from this **"space junk"**?

Teacher Information

IN THE SPOTLIGHT

Homework Central might sound like a train station you wouldn't want to stop at, but lots of links and a homework directory make this site well worth a visit. Click on its special feature, "Kid's spotlight," which has regular weekly features so there's always something new to see. You can also take your pick of interactive games and knowledge challenges on the full range of subjects.

Explore the FANTASTIC FOREST

Your fingertips tingle

FOREST ENTRANCE

CENTER VIEW

ENTRANCE TO FOREST

EXIT FROM FOREST

What makes a Forest Fantastic? You're ...

hidden creature or feature.

The maple leaves on

> Once you're in the "Spotlight" you can go to "Exploration" and play an adventure game called "Fantastic forest." Follow clues to find out where different creatures live.

www.homeworkcentral.com

WEB WATCH

Here's a tip for those who don't know their long division from their multiplication tables, or think pi is something you eat with cream! Take a look at the **Allmath Homepage** with interactive flash cards, worksheets, and a game room, as well as a chance to "Ask an expert" if you get stuck.

www.allmath.com

PLAY SCHOOL

Do you need to relax after all that homework? That's where **Funschool** comes in! Click on the "Spot" to choose from dozens of Java games for different levels, and you can play and learn at the same time. Choose the level you want to play at. You can even play at being the teacher by grading the games!

Join Bonnie and Will for the "Downhill challenge" in 5th and 6th grade games or, if you're a budding scientist, click on "Element lab."

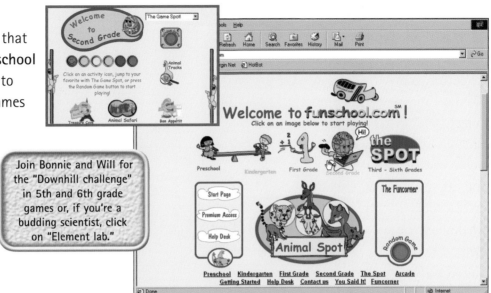

 www.funschool.com

IN THE CLASSROOM

Join Willy Wonka at the **Wonka School** for a choice of topics and games. You can send a "Wonkagram" to your friends! Click on "Willy's classroom" for a trivia quiz, or go to "Planet-o-matic" for some great games. Have you ever wondered how the internet works? Click on the "How it works" computer screen to find out! If you're looking for inspiration for school projects, it's also worth clicking on "Let's learn about..." or the "Library" to read about the book of the month.

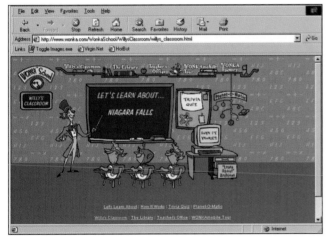

www.wonka.com

FUN AND GAMES

There's almost no text on the pages of **Alfy**'s amazing site, but icons talk when you click on them and the pictures make it easy to get around. Click on "Music mania" to play different musical instruments, or try out the alphabet circus and map race at the "Brain train." You can even see your own paintings hung in Alfy's museum at the "Club house," or click on "Arcade" to find lots of interactive games. Best of all, design your own Alfy homepage, with your favorite links to games, movies, chat rooms, and activities.

www.ALFY.com

HOT SPOTS

GAMES

Bonus.com	www.Bonus.com
Headbone	www.headbone.com/games
Heat	www.heat.com
Javagameplay.com	www.javagameplay.com
Kidscom Games	www.Kidscom.com
Kids Domain	www.kidsdomain.com
Microsoft Network Gaming Zone	www.zone.com
The Riddler	www.riddler.com
Virtual Arcade 1.0	www.thearcade.com
Yahooligans! Games	http://play.yahoo.com/yahooligans.html

VIRTUAL PLAYGROUND

Alfy – The Kids' Portal Playground	www.Alfy.com
Coolkid	www.coolkid.com
Cyberkids!	www.cyberkids.com
Kids' Place	www.eduplace.com/kids
Kids Play Safe	www.wawakwala.com
Kids' Space	www.kids-space.org
My MaMaMedia	www.mamamedia.com
Superstar Kids' Club	www.superstarkidsclub.com
Yuckiest Site on the Internet	www.yucky.com
Zeeks.com	www.zeeks.com

CHITCHAT

Cool Kids Chat	www.chat-wave.com/kids
FreeZone!	www.freezone.com
Girl Tech	www.girltech.com
Girl Zone	www.girlzone.com
Headbone Zone	www.headbonezone.com
Key Pals Club	www.mightymedia.com/keypals
Kid City Live Kids Chat	www.child.net/kcchat.htm
Kidscom Graffiti Wall	www.Kidscom.com
Kids World	www.kidsworld.org
World Village	www.worldvillage.com

HOMEWORK

BJ Pinchbeck	http://school.discovery.com/students/homeworkhelp/bjpinchbeck
Encarta Encyclopedia	http://encarta.msn.com
Encyclopedia.com from Electric Library	www.encyclopedia.com
ePlay – Homework Help	www.eplay.com/homework
Fun School	www.funschool.com
Homework Central	www.homeworkcentral.com
Kids Web	www.kidsvista.com/index.html
StudyWeb	www.studyweb.com
WordCentral	www.wordcentral.com
ZoomSchool	www.EnchantedLearning.com/school

KIDS SEARCHERS

AOL Search Kids Only	www.aol.com/netfind/kids
Ask Jeeves for Kids	www.ajkids.com
Berit's Best Sites for Children	www.beritsbest.com
The Go2Net Network	www.100hot.com/directory/lifestyles/kids.html
KidsClick!	http://sunsite.berkeley.edu/KidsClick!
KidsDomain	www.kidsdomain.co.uk
LycosZone	http://lycoszone.lycos.com
Net-mom Homepage	www.netmom.com
Smart Zones	http://home.edview.com
Yahooligans!	www.yahooligans.com

MUSIC

All Music Guide	www.allmusic.com
cbc4 Kids	www.cbc4kids.ca/general/music/default.html
Children's Music Web	www.childrensmusic.org
Children's Music Web Guide	http://cmw.cowboy.net/WebG/default.html
Garden State Pops Youth Orchestra	www.gspyo.com
Music Notes	http://library.thinkquest.org/15413
Paula Music	www.paulamusic.demon.co.uk
Piano on the Net	www.artdsm.com/music.html
PlayMusic!	www.playmusic.org
The Ultimate Band List	www.ubl.com

SENSATIONAL SPORTS

Baseball	www.fastball.com/playball
Exploratorium's Sports Science	www.exploratorium.edu
Football	www.playfootball.com
Foxsports.com	www.foxsports.com
Olympics	www.olympics.com/eng
The Locker Room	http://members.aol.com/msdaizy/sports/locker.html
The Mountain Zone	www.mountainzone.com
Sky Sports	www.skysports.com
Sports.com	www.sports.com
SportsForWomen.com	www.sportsforwomen.com
Sports Illustrated for Kids	www.sikids.com
Steven's Online Kids Sports Club	http://hometown.aol.com/Sftrail/steven.html
Tennis	www.tennis.com
Youth Sports Network	www.ysn.com

ENTERTAINMENT FILM & TV

Disney	www.disney.com
Entertainment Drive	www.edrive.com
The Force.net – Your Daily Dose of Star Wars	www.theforce.net
Imax	http://www.imax.com
Mr. Showbiz	http://mrshowbiz.go.com
MZTV Museum of Television	www.mztv.com
National Museum of Photography, Film, and Television	www.nmsi.ac.uk/nmpft
TeenHollywood.com	www.teenhollywood.com
Universal studios	www.universalstudios.com/fp.kids.html
Warner Bros. Kids Page	http://www.kids.warnerbros.com

SCIENCE & TECHNOLOGY

Astronomy for Kids	www.dustbunny.com/afk
Cool Science for Curious Kids	www.hhmi.org/coolscience
Discovery Online	www.discovery.com
The Exploratorium	www.exploratorium.edu
Fun Science Gallery	www.funsci.com
How Stuff Works	www.howstuffworks.com
Kids @ nationalgeographic.com	www.nationalgeographic.com/kids
Star Child	http://starchild.gsfc.nasa.gov/docs/StarChild/StarChild.html
World Wildlife Fund	www.wwf-uk.org/home.shtml
The Why Files	http://whyfiles.news.wisc.edu

WEIRD & WACKY

Aliens Aliens	www.mufor.org/aliens.htm
The Case.com	www.TheCase.com/kids
Guinness World Records	www.guinnessrecords.com
Illusion Works	www.illusionworks.com
Obiwan's UFO-Free Paranormal Page	www.ghosts.org
Pig Latin Converter	http://voyager.cns.ohiou.edu/~jrantane/menu/pig.html
Silly Putty	www3.hmc.edu/~jkurtze/sillyindex.htm
Stupid Candy	www.stupid.com
Wacky Patent of the Month	http://colitz.com/site/wacky.htm
The Weird Animal Express	http://tqjunior.advanced.org/5801

NETSPEAK

While on the internet, you may come across many alien words or terms that it is helpful to understand. Read this glossary and surfing the web will be smooth sailing!

Attachment Something extra - a sound or graphics file, for example - that you enclose with an email.

Bookmarks (or favorites) File used to store website addresses on your browser.

Browser Software that lets you surf, or browse, and read the web, moving between sites and pages.

Cache Part of the browser that automatically stores the text and images from pages you have visited recently. This means that you don't have to waste time downloading them again.

Chat Swap messages in real time (as you write them) with other people through an online forum (chat room). This is different from email because whatever you write can be read at the same time that you are writing it.

Cookie Calling card that some websites leave on your computer so that when you return they know who you are and what you looked at last time.

Crash The nightmare scenario when the screen freezes! You will probably need to reboot (restart) the computer.

Cyberspace Originally this word came from William Gibson's novel, *The Neuromancer*, and it has come to mean the whole world of chat, email, and everything else that's online.

Directory A site or search engine with links to a list of sites under different categories.

Domain name The part of an internet address (e.g dk.com) that lets you know who they are.

Download Copy a file from the internet onto your computer - not really any different from recording a CD or taping a video. Beware of big files that can take a long time.

Email (electronic mail) Put simply, the clue is in the name - sending and receiving files and text over the internet.

Emoticons When words aren't enough, all those face images used in chat and email :-)

FAQs Frequently asked questions (and, hopefully, most useful answers).

Favorites (See bookmarks)

File Anything stored on a computer, from text and pictures to sound and video.

Filter (or blocker) A piece of software used to keep out any unsuitable internet material.

Folder Where you keep your files or email messages - a sort of filing cabinet.

Homepage The first page you see when you visit a website, often with links to the contents of the website.

HTML (hypertext markup language) The language, or set of codes, used to format a webpage.

HTTP (hypertext transfer protocol) The code that identifies a webpage for the browser.

Hyperlink Hotspots that act as gateways from one page to another.

Interface This is what you see on the screen - the more icons and buttons to press, the more interactive the interface is.

Internet (Net) Well, in a few words, it's a network of interconnected computers. But then it's so much more!

ISDN Digital - and very speedy - phone connection.

ISP (Internet Service Provider) A company that gives you access to the internet.

Java (JavaScript) Advanced programming languages that can make standard html pages more impressive.

Modem Device that lets the computer dial up your ISP through the telephone connection.

MP3 A compressed audio format that allows you to download music to your computer.

Netiquette (and chatiquette) Take note! Rules and regulations about how to behave online.

Offline Not connected to the internet.

Online Connected to the internet.

Online Service A package that provides a connection, like an ISP, but also offers special features like chat rooms, newsgroups, and message boards.

Plug-in A program you can fit into your browser, often to let it download audio or video files.

PoP (point of presence) The telephone number your modem has to dial to get online.

Portal A site that acts as a directory, search engine, and general gateway onto the web.

Protocol A special language, or set of computer commands.

Search engine A database, or directory, that gives you links to specific sites throughout the web.

Server A central computer that provides the services for a network of (client) computers.

Spam All the unnecessary jokes and pictures that clog up the internet. Sometimes funny, but not often!

Streaming Audio or video files that play as you download them, not after.

Surfing The web equivalent of channel hopping.

URL (uniform resource locator) The address of any webpage.

Web (www - World Wide Web) The whole network of pages and sites on the internet.

Webpage A single document within a website.

Web ring A group of sites that are about a similar topic and share similar interests.

Website A collection of webpages all brought together under the homepage and connected by hyperlinks.

HELP!

For more jargon-busting, take a look at some of these online dictionaries:

The Jargon File www.jargon.org
PC Webopaedia www.pcwebopaedia.com
What Is www.whatis.com

THE FUTURE

You don't need a crystal ball to know that there's one word you had better get used to, and that's "digital." Digital is the opposite of analogue - and it's the key to 21st century web-surfing where everything is about speed.

Greater speed means better graphics and faster downloads, and that's what the digital revolution is promising. With digital technology, logging onto the web could be just as much of a thrill as walking into a 3-D cinema, with graphics, animations, and audio effects getting bigger, better, sharper, and more realistic all the time.

That's where cable comes in. With a digital fiber-optic cable connection you can download at up to 10Mbps (that's 10,000,000 bytes per second) compared to the normal 56Kbps (56,000 bytes per second) you get with a standard modem. At that kind of speed, virtual reality could soon be so fast, and interactive features so realistic, you will hardly be able to tell what's real and what's not. So much so that tele-immersion may finally become possible - where the gamer puts on a cyber suit or steps into a tele-cubicle and "enters" the game world itself!

Games aren't the only thing to change – the internet is hitting the streets and getting mobile. Forget text-messaging on your mobile, the whole of the net is about to go mobile. With the advent of WAP (Wireless Application Protocol) mobile phones, you will be able to go online, any time, any place.

It might be a few years before you see kids strolling down the street playing online games against opponents from the other side of the world, but mobile computing is a real possibility, and so are public internet facilities. E-phone booths, like the Citspace i-plus kiosks, are already springing up on street corners all over the world from which you'll soon find yourself sending emails, downloading and playing games, and shopping.

Developments in speed and mobility are waiting to shape the future. Whether it's the internet on TV, or audio-file transfer letting DJs fill dance floors from home, the possibilities are endless.

INDEX

Animals 32-35
Art 42-43
Blocking 4-5
Browsers 6
Browsing 6, 10-11
Chat rooms 17
Connecting 4-7
Creating websites 9, 14-15
Dinosaurs 35
the Earth 48-51

Email 16-17
Entertainment 20-31
Films 24-27
Games 20-23
Geography 44-51
History 38-41
Homepages 7, 8-9
Homework help 56-59
Hyperlinks 7
Insects 36-37
ISP (Internet Service Provider) 6

Jargon 14, 17, 62-63
Music 24-27
Nature 32-37
Netiquette 17,18-19
Safety 4-5, 7
School 9, 15
Search engines 6, 8, 11, 12-13
Space 52-53
Sports 28-30
Toolbar 8,10
Travel 44-47